THE SECURELY CONFERRED, VOUCHSAFED
KEEPSAKES OF MAERY S.

By Sibyl Kempson

53rd State Press
new writing for performance

53 SP 50
December 2024
Brooklyn, NY

The Securely Conferred, Vouchsafed Keepsakes of Maery S.
© Sibyl Kempson 2024
53rdstatepress.org

ISBN Number: 978-1737025511
Library of Congress Number: 2022948676

Book design: Chris Giarmo
Cover design: Chris Giarmo with Amanda Villalobos
Printed on recycled paper in the United States of America.

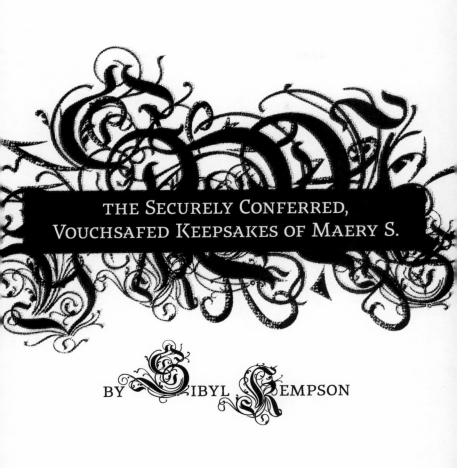

THE SECURELY CONFERRED, VOUCHSAFED KEEPSAKES OF MAERY S.

BY SIBYL KEMPSON

In loving memory of Joanne Jacobson

INTRODUCTION
BY KARINNE KEITHLEY SYERS

There's an exigency to Sibyl Kempson's very weird, very wild work, and I always feel better around it. Like many powerful thinkers who heed their own imperatives, Sibyl has no time for the existing valuations of what is high or low in our culture, and a real love of intelligent abundance wherever it occurs. Although her work doesn't bother with conformity to any mainstream rules, my sense is that her interests are not driven by experimentalism as a formal refusal or critique (in the sense of staking out a critical space external to the normative in order to speak to the normative) but rather atavistically medicinal, exercising a kind of atavism that can happily skate the surfaces of the present. She trawls the artifacts of recent decades with a net and ties them, as so many tin cans, to her own damn tail, before diving back toward the root through a fissure in the ground (probably somewhere in Pennsylvania). Sibyl's energies tend toward the deep-time values of theater: getting in the room, experiencing collective energy as an act of emanation, exhaustion, and repair. I want to say words like *vegetal* and *medicinal* when I think of her plays. I want to fly a flag and call people over. I once asked Sibyl about her approach to singing and she told me her job was "to put the song in the people." It struck me as a figure for a blood transfusion, apposite in that somehow what I get when I experience the sheer performative force of Sibyl's plays is counterpart to iron, to potassium, to the basic fact of immunity—something that allows our bodies to act on their own behalf but that also records and recollects a communal, social-physical gift inheritance.

That sense of mission to be a spelunker of our various minor forms of inherited knowledge about how to live—and how to bear living in what humans have made—is evident in this play with songs now attempting to occupy, in some of its dimensions, this book in your hands. Sibyl's plays have always engaged with excess and often with the gleeful ventriloquism of existing forms of dramatic literature (the semi-unintelligible old English curse, the expressionistic Bergman film, the collected Springsteen ballads), but *Maery S.* possesses an anti-(non?- skew?)-chronological sense of direction I'm still trying to wrap my head around. It seems to move in multiple, simultaneous pathways along both its timelines and its latitudinal lines. This has something to do with a perception of confluence and transmission that flows across minor literatures and commonly dismissed forms of speech (like, say, a comment stream on a Bigfoot site that still manifests the shapes and colors of internet 1.0, the one with neither commerce nor algorithm) that allows Sibyl to fold distributed planes into each other's edges. Merging the life of Mary Shelley, Shelley's *Frankenstein*, years of Bigfoot research, stages of the Gothic, the figure of Doris Duke, river landscapes of Germany and America (with their campingplatzes and rest stops), the play asks, "Why shouldn't I write of monsters?"

It has been years since I've been in the room of this play, but I've still got a trace map of its waterways in me. I got to be there for a few of its convenings, once at New Dramatists, where it gained its songs, and again at BAC, where it started to look for its feet and bodies. What remains for me are the impressions of two monsters. One, carried as a figure in a landscape by the overlaid figure of Frankenstein's monster and Sasquatch (who has always been running after your car down a dirt road somewhere in the middle of New Jersey). This monster is body, longing, a thing attempting to divine its own desires, a navigational being who refuses our entrapment by compass and so takes on the feeling of a threat. The other monster body is one made of fen-mist, made of the sorrow-fog rising out of the accumulated losses of agency endured by female bodies, especially in this case the ones in the circle around the real Maery S., cutting her path of (again, I can't help this verb or choose a different one) refusal. The present absence. ("All the children in our entourage are ghosts.") We were all in the room at New Dramatists — Sibyl's collaborators and gathered playwright residents—and the subject of all the women's ghost babies, whether stillborn or born out of wedlock and so forced into removal to a convent, was resonating. The great seer Sharon Bridgforth was in the room (she and Sibyl were two of the five playwrights working in the building simultaneously) and she asked, "How do the ghost babies serve the structure in the same way that the songs do?" I don't remember. Was it all the songs the chorus of ghost children sing, was it the dirge that followed? All of it? Something bloomed then. Song as a hinge point that folds around an edge. And the play dropped into gear.

When she was at BAC, I asked Sibyl what she was drawing on to put the play on its feet. She unspooled a wide-ranging set of sources, all of which in some way forms that face terror as both an internal and external form of confrontation: "The psychothriller of the 1970s ... the idea of the empty house ... something is in the house, and you don't know what ... films like *Klute, Don't Look Now, The Sentinel, The Wicker Man, The Changeling,* and particularly *The Driver's Seat,* based on Muriel Spark's late-career short story... Television shows I was vaguely remembering from when I was growing up and watching a lot of weird TV in the late seventies that basically scared the living crap out of me, permanently... The prologue to James Whale's film *The Bride of Frankenstein* from 1935 ... a LOT of YouTube video footage of Bigfoot sightings, and other YouTube videos of guys analyze those sightings, as well as more fully-produced documentaries on the subject ... Tours that you get to go on sometimes of old homes that have been taxidermied and turned into stuffy museums. The LBJ library in Austin. The Crook House in Omaha. Edwin Booth's room at the Players Club. Graceland! Stroud Mansion. The Isabella Stewart Gardner Museum in Boston. Duke Farms! Southfork Ranch! ... Places where I've hiked and camped in the Rheinsteig region of Germany. The style is in the topography there, gentle and severe at the same time, long-civilized but it hasn't forgotten its pre-Christian wildness and still honors it by what has been preserved through time."

Reader, I am inadequate to introduce this play. I'm glad you are reading it. It is so funny and it is also terribly sad and also its motor never stops.

Reader, I hope this play comes to feel to you, as it does to me, like a kind of possession, a thing that doesn't leave you, a memory on your edges that decoheres something in you while at the same time dropping a perfect, silent plumb line into your deeps.

Reader, watch out for the wild night pigs.

LIST of CHARACTERS:

WITNESS 1 / GROUNDSKEEPER 1

WITNESS 2 / GROUNDSKEEPER 2

MAERY S. / FANNY / CLARIE, OR CLAIRE

MRS. WILLS, "COOK" / LB / DAEMONUS CERAMICI /
    LEFT PEASANT MAID / REST AREA PAINTER

LADY DUKE / RIGHT PEASANT MAID / JANE / PERCY

MONSTER

INSIDE the "STORY":

TIME and PLACE ARE FLUID and WONKY. THEY INCLUDE ...

ASSORTED EUROPEAN NATIONS IN THE 19th CENTURY:

- DARK, BUT COZY HEARTH of the GODWIN RESIDENCE on SKINNER STREET, LONDON
- GERMANY'S RHEINSTEIG, DURING BOTH GOTHIC ERAS & ALSO DURING the PRESENT DAY
- NURSERY, in ASSORTED TEMPORARY EUROPEAN RESIDENCES
- CAMPINGPLATZ am MITTELRHEIN und RHEINSTEIG
- AUF DEM RüDEL

ASSORTED UNITED STATES, 1970S TO 2000S:

- A COLLEGIATE LECTURE HALL
- A BACK ROAD
- ASSORTED TRUCK STOPS and REST AREAS along the U.S. INTERSTATE
- DUKE ESTATE GROUNDS with TERRARIUM and CONSERVATORY
- DUKE ESTATE INTERIOR, DIVIDED into USED and UNUSED PORTIONS by a DRESSER-BLOCKED DOOR. IN SOME CASES, THIS INTERIOR is ONLY SEEN FROM THE EXTERIOR.

HERE ARE SOME AREAS OF NOTE:

THE WITNESS STATION, A SAFE HAVEN WHERE WITNESSES CAN RECORD THEIR EXPERIENCES AND INVESTIGATORS CAN REPORT THEIR FINDINGS. IT HAS MEGAPHONES MADE OUT OF CARDBOARD, DESKTOP COMPUTER, SHOEBOX RECORDER WITH SMALL MICROPHONE, LOG BOOK, ANALOG TELEPHONE RECEIVERS, BALES OF HAY, AND SONY WALKMEN. THERE IS A SCROLLING TICKER-TAPE-TYPE NEWSFEED WITH IMAGES IN VIDEO ABOVE.

A LARGE MAP (A "MAPESTRY"), SHEWING THE VARIOUS GEOGRAPHICAL AREAS ON WHICH THE ACTION OF THE PLAY TAKES PLACE. THE MAP IS ANIMATED AND HAS THE CAPABILITY OF SHEWING FIGURES MOVING UPON IT, AND LIGHTS UP IN DIFFERENT SECTIONS VIA COLOURED PEGS, AS IN A LITE-BRITE®. AS WITH THE FONDLY-REMEMBERED LITE BRITE®, ITS BLACK BACKGROUND PAPER IS REPLACED NOW AND AGAIN, WITH NEW IMAGES OF GEOGRAPHIES INTRODUCED AS THEY FIGURE IN TO THE PLOT.

A DOUBLED SLASH ("//") INDICATES AN INSTANCE WHEREIN THE SUCCEEDING SPEAKER INTERRUPTS THE PRESENT ONE.

ᥰ🕮 *INDEX OF SONGS* 🕮ᥱ

⇒ PART 1 ⇐

THE DIVULGENT STRATA

*But listen! – at the very first crack of dawn, the ground
Underfoot began to mutter, the woody ridges to quake,
And a baying of hounds was heard through the half-light:
the goddess was
Coming.*

      Hecate.

             - The Aeneid

1. The Tail End of an Introductory Presentation (Just What Exactly Are We Dealing With Here?)

We enter into a dry, fluorescent-lit, industrial-carpeted collegiate lecture hall. Or perhaps one of the old ones with wooden seats and wrought-iron railings, entered from a foyer of marble, with bronze fixtures and busts of 'the greats.'

On the projection screen: a fractured and altered video montage of early home movies of the Duke Estate, the architectures of Princeton and Duke University and the ruins of several late Gothic Rhineland fortresses, morphing in and out of the bulleted points of a powerpoint presentation. All is morphing and moving, and snippets of sound throughout the history of Dark Romanticism, technological exploration, the transformations of Ancient Greece, and of modern Bigfoot research, can be heard from within a maelstrom of experience that surrounds and envelops the small audience as they enter and find their seats.

There is also a MAPESTRY, which is animated and illuminated, displaying several flashing travel routes throughout various time periods in the United States and Europe. These routes are illuminated by turns, in colored pegs that have been poked through the black paper background.

And then, lights out!

And lights up again!

On a lady. A Lady.

A lady who has been giving a presentation in this room the whole time, but on another level of reality. (There will be a lot of that going on in this piece. Buckle up.) She is The Lady Jane Doris Duke, philanthropist, heiress, collector. Widow. Well-aged and meticulously preserved. The presentation she has been giving has been an introductory presentation.

LADY DUKE:
And so, I would like to conclude by saying:
This people had been better left alone by the transformations of civilization, the literatures and musics—and left in the deep brooding innocence of barbarianism, believing that same sparkling water on the surface of the mighty river was what ran in their veins, not the spurting red schluck that Maery S. would later gulp like so much Christmastide Glühwein, //
and which ran down the windows of the burg castle schlosses and stained the solemn stones for eternity, gushing down the steep slopes onto the historically infallible blacksmiths in the villages, bungling and delaying their work. Better off without the tortures of art and literature and philosophy that crazed them so irrevocably.

MAERY:
(From a deeply recessed corner)
// Yeah! Yeah! Yeah! // Yeah! Yeah!

LADY DUKE:
// Maery, please!

The interjection is from Maery S., a version of Mary Shelley. (There are several – one for each definition of the word "Gothic.") This one has been lurking in the deeply recessed corner, snuggling an unusual wooden box-desk protectively to herself. She cradles and rocks it back and forth, to and fro, lifting its lid a little bit to peer inside. The box emits, onto the video screen, a scramble of commissioned portraits of the circle of free-thinkers whose lives and philosophies precede our story. Godwin, Coleridge, Shelley, Byron, Wollstonecraft Godwin Shelley.

At the same time, several routes along the MAP light up and are flashing.

LADY DUKE:
And that was only one of the parts of her. For there really was one for every definition of the word "Gothic."

The video montage screen now hones in on the portraits of Mary Shelley, photographs of her signature on letters, and during the following they morph into palimpsests of Old Gothic runes, and castle ruins morph into strange druidic-looking dolmen-type structures and rock formations.

Then, with a certain exasperation at having to repeat herself to the audience, who, as she perceives them, are latecomers to the presentation:

LADY DUKE:
(*Heavy, forceful sigh*)
I'm afraid you are late (I don't know *what* took you so long), and all we'll have time for, unfortunately, is the tail end of my introductory presentation. Please take your seats as quickly and quietly as possible.

She waits, in an attitude of martyrdom, leaning on the console with both hands, for the disturbances of coats, bodies, and belongings that she perceives to settle. Then, admonishing the audience with a severe look,
She sings.

ᥫᩚ *SONG: I'VE GOT THE BOX* ᥫᩚ

I am Lady Doris Duke.
You may please to call me Lady Duke
or, "The Lady Duke."
Or Lady Jane also.
Lady Jane Williams Duke.

(She speaks)
For now. I've provided generous funding for what you
are to experience this evening, thanks to the vast tobacco
and electric energy fortune to which I have been heiress,
to my philanthropic pursuits and my avocation and true
calling as avid Collector of art, horticulture, fauna, and other
objets d'intéresse.

(She sings)
In fact it was *through* my collecting that I came to know
Mary's famous box desk. To know, for me, is to *collect,*

(She speaks)
in fact, and I am most famous for my many collections.

(She sings)
And so that is how I am here today. Originally it was Muriel
Spark who was meant to give the lecture today.

(She speaks)
Very sorry, Muriel: you may be the expert,

(She sings)
but I've got the *Box.*

• ᥫᩚ

(Speaking now, to Maery)
Maery, maybe not to snuggle the Box so tightly so that other people, our guests, for instance, can have a look at the contents …?

She reaches for the Box with the intention to display and bandy it about triumphantly, but Maery resists, snuggling it protectively to herself. They struggle briefly.

LADY DUKE:
Inconvenient. In the same way of the spirits from some original geography hovering around the *collected* artifacts housed safely and respectfully in, say, the British Museum … Ahem! Very good. And so, if we may continue. On a little drive, down Exposition Boulevard …

The powerpoint screen, meanwhile, has become a scramble of commissioned portraits of the circle of free-thinkers whose lives and philosophies precede our story. Godwin, Wollstonecraft, Coleridge, Shelley, Byron, Wollstonecraft Godwin Shelley. The Lady Duke expounds them and their respective biographical storylines, which are animated on the screen.

LADY DUKE:
Ahem. So. Mary Wollstonecraft, the great and valiant proto-Feminist, who, along with her illegitimate infant daughter Fanny, came to live with William Godwin, Wollstonecraft's free-thinking yet good-hearted paramour, when she learned she would birth another child by Godwin. Tragically, Wollstonecraft died as a result of the difficult birth of this second daughter, named also Mary. This is *our* Mary. Aggrieved and suddenly left alone with two infant daughters, Godwin quickly and thoughtlessly took up with a second wife who brought her own daughter to the mix, Clare, whom our Maery calls Clarie. It's not in any of the documentation. Fine. And the

swirl of boy geniuses and devotees of Godwin's radical theories
of free thought, and of the girls' exuberant charms (well, not
Fanny's) and precocious intelligence (well, not Claire's), would
nearly make the home a merry one, had it not been for this
second Mrs. Godwin who steered the ship away from the
heights of giddy intellectualism and into the perils of trade,
// and one brilliant genius Percival /// Bysshe Shelley, who
managed to sweep all three girls directly off their feet.

MAERY:
// That bookshoppe. So dreary.

MAERY:
/// It was just Percy. Not Percival.

LADY DUKE:
(Cont'd)
Maery? Do you have anything you would like to add? Please be
specific. Any anecdotes are especially appreciated.

MAERY:
(Counting off on fingers, a shopping list)
I marry what is other-than-human inside myself.
(But it's maybe a different one than everybody thinks it is.)
I'm doing all the work.
I'm making this whole show happen.
I'm still just the one person.
(Which is the situation we choose when we marry outside of
human inside ourself.)
I don't have a mother. I woke up in the backseat and looked in
the front seat and there was no mother there to drive the car!!!
How was the car driving itself!?

LADY DUKE:
There, there, Maery. There, there, now.

(To the audience)
Notice the angular style, the broad vertical downstrokes?
That'll be **the lettering, 13ᵗʰ Century, including Fraktur and blackletter typefaces**.
Bet you she's got some in there –
(To Maery)
How about letting us have a look inside the Box, Maery?
(To the audience)
I've managed to ensure that all of the original relics are intact.
There are many letters, identifications, validations,
and inclusions—
(Maery pulls out some stacks of these items)
a notebook she shared with Percy Bysshe Shelley, with a copy
of his poem "Adonaïs" with one page folded around a silk parcel
containing some of his ashes and the remains of his heart.
And locks of all her children's hair, including that of the many
who died in infancy, and the one that lived …

*Maery pulls out a very long piece of dark fur that keeps coming
out and coming out. It is unexpected and surprises and disturbs
them both.*

LADY DUKE:
Oh. And …

*Maery glares at The Lady Duke, who stares back uncomfortably.
And the fur keeps coming.*

*The sound of the engine of a pickup truck shifting into a
lower gear in order to get up a hill. The lights in the lecture
hall are flickering.*

LADY DUKE:
(Nervously)
Ladies and Gentlemen, kind colleagues, there seems to be some
kind of electrical problem. Not surprising.

(*Sighs, decides to come to terms*)
When we truthfully consider Mary Shelley, it is true that we
must consider *all* versions of her ...
Throughout history,
recurring, returning,
herself and each of her sisters.
Each a manifestation of one of the faces of the Moon, Earth,
and Underworld.
Each a living face of myriad ancestries.
Abducted and absconded in youth & virginity.

MAERY:
Don't forget:
She who works her will.
She who harnesses the magical energies of clay.
She who brings the coolness of night to the scorched land.
She who hastens the birth.
Creatrix of the Cosmos even ...
She who encounters you.
She who is all that has been and all that will be.

LADY DUKE:
No mortal has ever lifted her Veil—not even *me!*

MAERY:
Wisdom of dark places and Warrior Goddess of crossroads,
levels of knowledge.
With my sisters: both surface and depth of oceans, wheel of the
year, web of fate.
Virgin Huntress, Psychopomp,
residing in the other plane.

LADY DUKE:
Veiled and beyond the Veil,
pale and beyond the pale,

never plain on the other plane,
She goes and has gone by many names ...

MAERY:
Selene.[1] Artemis.[2] Mawu.[3] Arawa.[4] Andriamahilala.[5]
Arianrhod.[6] Ngame.[7] Yemaya.[8] Olókun.[9] Oshun.[10] Metztli.[11]
Olapa.[12] Persephone, or Kore.[13] Cerridwen.[14] Anahita.[15]
Ataensic.[16] Hekate. Hecate.[17] Isis, even. All. All.

1. Titan Moon goddess of Greek mythology.

2. Olympian goddess of Greek mythology associated with the Moon.

3. Beninese Moon goddess, female and male on either side of her body.

4. Moon goddess of Suk and Pokot tribes of Kenya and Uganda.

5. Malagasy first woman and Moon goddess, who populated the Earth with humans and then went to the Moon to rest.

6. Celtic Moon goddess whose name means "Silver Wheel" – of the year and web of fate.

7. Akan (of Ghana) triple goddess of the soul and the Moon, creatrix of celestial planets.

8. Yorùbá Orisha representing the surface of the Ocean, source of all Waters, and in Santería the Ocean Mother to all the Fish, and in Haitian Vodou, the goddess of the Moon.

9. Sister Orisha to Yemaya, who represents the depths of the Ocean and dreams. Together the sisters form a balance.

10. In Nigerian Yorùbá tradition, River goddess, spirit of Sweet Water, Orisha of Love and Romance.

11. Aztec goddess of the Moon.

12. Moon goddess of the Maasai.

13. Greek goddess of vegetation, ruling the Underworld together with her husband Hades, who abducted and raped her as a way of beginning a relationship.

14. Welsh Moon goddess.

15. Persian goddess of Venus and the Moon, known as the "immaculate one" representing the cleansing and fertilizing flow of the Cosmos.

16. North American First Nations' Sky Woman.

17. Triple-form Grecian goddess of Moon, Earth, and Underworld, also crossroads, entrance-ways, night, magic, and witchcraft.

The Lady Duke, fascinated, attempts to reach into the Box.
Maery slams it shut.

LADY DUKE:
Ow, my FINGEHS! Maery!

Maery slips away ...

LADY DUKE:
(*Chasing after her*)
Maery! Come back here! Come back here with that Box! Maery!

The crashing chords of a piano raze the mood. DAEMONUS
CERAMICI delivers the Program Note.

PROGRAM NOTE, A SONG-POEM.

Please welcome to enter, please
A tribute to the rivers and their tributaries.
The Rhine, Mississippi, and Passaic
in especial.
To the hills above these rivers,
that tell and re-tell the deepest and oldest
stories to those who are apt to listen.
Please welcome to enter, please
A tribute to the roads of the United States
and to interstate journeys, and to those
who do not fear to travel from one state [of being] state [of
mind] into another.
Into another, into another.
A tribute to all the definitions of "Gothic."
Goths.
Goth.
Gothic.
Gothick.
Please welcome to enter, please
A tribute to the monsters we are,
the monsters within, the monsters we birth,
and the monsters we make.
This tribute is a sewn-together and re-animated
aberration made of discarded and unwanted imaginative
excess.
To those who have seen the unexplainable,
and those who then try to explain what they saw.
We salute you.

The lights fade to darkness, all but the overhead lightbulb at the Witness Station. Over their next page or so of lines, even that fades to total darkness. After a while, our eyes adjust, and we see that Maery stands near the witness stand. Her Box Desk is attached to her body like the tray of a cigarette girl. The Witnesses are passing their testimonies to her and putting them in the slot at the top of her Box Desk. The places described are illuminated on the MAP. While this is happening, Maery weeps silently. Each place must represent some distant regret.

2. OPENING TESTIMONY. CLASS A.

WITNESS 1: My husband and I were on our way home last fall on a main road near a bridge which crosses over Possum Creek around 11 p.m. on a rainy night, coming around a curve next to the Chickamauga Lake.[18]

WITNESS 2: My husband and I were driving home on I-75, the day after Christmas.

WITNESS 1: My husband and I were on a motorcycle ride to Siloam Springs State Park. We were driving about 40 to 45 miles per hour coming down a hill.

WITNESS 2: My fiancee and I were We were headed up to the hill to park at our favorite makeout spot—

WITNESS 1: We were on a dirt road.

WITNESS 2: Hi, I am 47 years old and I am a truck driver. I had an eye Witness of something yesterday January 16, 2013 in Clark Co. Ill.

WITNESS 1: It was about 2 months ago, I was coming home from taking my sister home after we got out of work

18. The vast majority of Witness testimonies throughout the play (with the exception of Witness 3) are quoted verbatim from reported sightings on BFRO. net. Used with permission from the BFRO.

WITNESS 2: To the right there is a steep hill that had a lot of trees and obstacles.

WITNESS 1: As we reached the top, we saw the full moon and it lit up a flat green pasture that was on top of the hill.

WITNESS 2: It starts off winding through woods and while curving to the right

WITNESS 1: it was spring 1981 and I was driving around some country roads with a friend listening to music when the tape jammed. I pulled over to fix it but left the car running & headlights on. I looked up from the tape & saw the bushes moving on the opposite side of the road,

WITNESS 2: And heading north, just after I made the turn and fumbling with my coffee cup, something caught my eye!

WITNESS 1: when I noticed something.

WITNESS 2: I looked up and saw

WITNESS 1: As soon as I looked out I saw

WITNESS 2: I turned to look and was shocked to see

WITNESS 1: was looking thru my binoculars when something came out

WITNESS 2: I wasn't ready to see what i saw and to this day my hair stands on end when i tell this

WITNESS 1: I seen something out of the corner of my eye wich until I had turned my head

WITNESS 2: in the field about 200-300 yards away ...

WITNESS 1: Suddenly, my brother shouted and I looked ahead

WITNESS 2: I saw ... something ... cross the highway going from south to north about 500 meters in front of me.

WITNESS 1: Something walked to my window, almost totally blocking the moonlight, and looked in.

WITNESS 1: I stood there in amazement just looking at it.

WITNESS 2: I threw back the covers, and whipped around to look at the windows as I got out of bed.

WITNESS 1: Then I realize it's not a haystack.

WITNESS 2: I could see it clearly in the brakelights and some light coming from a lodge across the road

WITNESS 1: I was too chicken to get any closer than i was.

WITNESS 2: This watching went on for less than a minute

WITNESS 1: The strange thing is that we didn't talk about what we saw, but just acted together knowing we couldn't explain it.

WITNESS 2: My friend said that he was walking his dog in the same place and his dog started to bark like crazy at something.

WITNESS 1: I wanted to run down the hall and get the grownups

WITNESS 2: When I realized what I was seeing I instintly crouched out of view

WITNESS 1: My heart and breathing lost rhythm, and shock prevented me from moving normally. Decisions and memory felt distorted and everything raced through my mind. I asked myself over and over, did that just happen? DID THAT JUST HAPPEN?

WITNESS 2: She looked up and saw what they were scream-ing about

WITNESS 1: As we made the turn to the right/south I noticed a big figure standing.

WITNESS 2: As we made the turn to the right/south I noticed a big figure standing.

We are in total darkness. Crickets. All around us are footsteps. Something is circling our campsite—something bipedal and very, very large. We hear leaves and sticks crunching beneath its heavy, circling steps. A few splashes as if some large rocks or bricks are dumped into swampy water, then the sounds of a large creature wading. Bullfrogs. Wind through the boughs of large trees. It is still very, very dark.

Suddenly, a terrible scream.

The sounds of the forest, the swamp, the mountains all die away. Only the scream remains, until it spends itself into a terrible, low moan, groans, turns mournful, and dies out.

The chime of a very old clock. The crackle and snap of a fire. The slow rhythmic creaking of a rocking chair.

LADY DUKE:
(*Sneaking covertly into the new scene from the previous scene*)
The Godwin's house on Skinner Street, in London, where
the girls grew to adolescence, under the watchful eye of one
Mrs. Wills, forgotten in the history books and also known as
"Cook." She is here in the rocking chair, at the edge of darkness,
struggling to preserve the boundaries.
For here we shall learn that the adolescent sisters FANNY,
CLARIE, and MAERY are plotting a rebellious elopement
abroad with the already-famous, already-married great
Romantic poet Percy Shelley. Old Mrs. Wills's got her work
cut out for her keeping the turbulent exuberance of these girls
from toppling over every societal structure man has struggled
to build since the Roman Empire ...

*Clarie arrives first, with an overhanging lantern, which further
lights the scene. Fanny enters, with a regrettable and depressed
slouch. Both girls are taking turns kissing a portrait that Claire is
carrying.*

LADY DUKE:
(*Cont'd*)
Our stepsisters Clarie and Fanny are worshipping a portrait
of Percy Bysshe Shelley. In it he is sitting in front of a fine
example of:

(Now she is in the lecture hall again)

> **The prevalent-in-Western-Europe style of architecture –**
> **GOTHIC – 12th to 16th centuries. Note the pointed arches, the**
> **ribbed vaults, flying buttresses, you know the look – large**
> **windows. Elaborate tracery. I believe this portrait was**
> **painted posthumously by one Joseph Severn ... I wonder**
> **how they got a hold of it ...**

COOK:
(Interrupting)
All will have the health-giving broth. Who will have pudding?

Pause. No answer.

LADY DUKE:
(Stepping back into the hearth scene, unable to help herself)
Ah, Cook, of whom there is no record of having lived in the
debt-ridden Godwin household at any time (as I've mentioned,
except for a few scant references to a mysterious "Mrs. Wills").
Note the ancient fireplace that is more like a cave: (I think it's
the same one they used for *Wuthering Heights*!)

*Fanny and Clarie sit reluctantly before it in chairs and take up
wooden tobacco pipes while Cook, Mrs. Wills, stirs and stirs ...*

The girls wiggle about in their chairs, smoking and plotting.

COOK:
WHO WILL HAVE PUDDING. ALL WILL HAVE BROTH.

LADY DUKE:
(Cont'd)
They were always a handful, these girls, full of ideas and
schemata, bubbling in gaiety, conversation, intellect ...

COOK:

And where is Maery? I expected her return from the gravestones of the cemet'ry by night's fall. And ... it is night.

MAERY:

(*Giggling*)

I was at the St. Pancras Cemetery, visiting my mother's grave, and as Claire put it:

(*Putting on a ravenous and reckless impression of Clarie*)

"Having a hump. Right on top of the gravestone and among her schoolbooks!"

COOK:

Broth's not optional. Ett.

MAERY:

I was sixteen. I think. We never kept track of my birthday very well because it was the same day as my mother died. One of the reasons I visited her grave so much was to check and see how old I was. Fanny was nineteen or twenty by then. A spinster and a gloomy one. "Did you see her there, Clarie?" Always wanting proof.

COOK:

Ett your broth, girls.

(*Grumbling under her breath*)

Don't want any part anything any one these girls is up to. Just to put in a good day's work and get on with it.

(*To Clarie*)

Clarie, ett your broth.

MAERY:

Clarie wouldn't answer and wouldn't eat.

COOK:
Stoke the fire, then. Fanny, stoke the fire.

Silence. Fanny stokes the fire. The old clock tocks.

Fanny fetches another log. Flumps it onto the pile of other burning logs. Watches the fire crackle up.

Clarie stares hungrily at the fire.

MAERY:
"Not hungry, Claire?" Fanny could never resist stoking the coals.
And Claire was "'ungry all right, but not for broth ... "

COOK:
(*Wanting all this to stop so she doesn't have to take responsibility to stop it herself*)
Smoke your pipe, then. Quiet down and smoke y' pipe.

Cook smokes her pipe, to demonstrate.

Clarie smokes her pipe, to temporarily obey.

Fanny smokes her pipe, to follow along.

Cook turns away to ladle the curdled pudding. She is very dense and heavy, much like the pudding itself, and her movements require a greater effort than those of most, as if she is subject to the gravity on a planet of much greater mass than Earth.

Fanny, disgusted with Claire, grabs the portrait and has a long kiss with it to console herself and then puts it away in the darkness before Mrs. Wills can see. Many moments pass without anything else.

The clock chimes dully.

The chair rocks. A silent invitation arrives to deep contemplation.

MAERY:
(*Bringing bowls, aside*)
Claire always disgusted Fanny very deeply. Bad behavior is one
thing, but nasty manners to boot. And yet, Fann couldn't keep
it inside any longer:
(*As Fanny*)
"And HE was there with her? My darling Shelley ..."
(*Aside*)
for we all three were in love with him. Clarie was always ready,
and shot back:
(*As Clarie*)
"YOUR Shelley! Puh! And saying such things to MAERY
like 'Darling.' 'October moon.' 'United, intimate.' 'Magnificent
natures creature!' 'Ardent passion!' 'O treasure - consent!
Consent!'
(*Aside*)
He really did say all those things, so that's accurate! It was that
night that Clarie decided to tattle our plans to Cook, as an act
of especial cruelty:
(*As Clarie*)
"Soon enough we'll be running away from here, on a journey,
you know, Cook."
(*Aside*)
And she told everything, so that once we'd taken flight Cook'd
have to keep the secret together with Fanny – who was (yikes!)
not invited on the journey.
(*As Clarie*)
"And you're not to breathe a word of it to Father or Mother!"

COOK:
(*Thickly, resigned*)
Pudding's cu'ddled.

MAERY:

Father would desperately want me back, but Claire's mother wouldn't. If Father could scrape together any money – he wouldn't – he'd send out a search party to arrest us, so we knew to throw our virginity to the winds first thing. And I was privy to the real meaning of virginity which is:

(*From the cemetery, over the baying of hounds on the ridge in the distance*)

Nothing. It's utterly meaningless. I have it from my own mother, from beyond her grave.

The very grave on which I was now absorbing the tremendous feelings of the great and almighty Romantic poet of our time as my chosen phallus bearer (and Claire's, and Fanny's), throbbing heart-throb.

(*As Clarie*)

"Who did not choose Fanny, of course. Sorry, Fann."

(*As Fanny*)

"Or you ... "

(*Aside*)

Fanny was quick to point out to Claire.

(*As Clarie*)

"Yet. Not YET,"

(*Aside*)

corrected Clarie, looking for a moment a little like a frantic pig. As for me, it was the first crack of dawn here in the church-yard. Everything I needed was there. Mother, lover, and ... somebody ... something ... else ... which I can't yet see, but which is – gurgling in the womb of the grave!!!

COOK:

You girls ...

(*Sings, breaking the spell*)

You girls, you girls.
Think your own life is beginning to open up scene by scene,
vista by greater vista.
You girls, you girls, I remember how it is.
Like those little Ukrainian dolls in the nursery.
You girls, you girls. You'll tear them open only to find they get
smaller instead.
You girls, you girls. What's more, you'll spend the rest of
your lives
trying to fit those empty halves together again,

(*Speaks*)
As in your haste cracking them open you miss the way their
originality assemblage.

(*Sings*)
SO, you girls, you girls,
go smoke your pipe
and ett your broth
and quiet down. Quiet down. Quiet down.

• 🪰

MAERY:
(*As Clarie*)
You might not think me so fancy, but I can step into a carriage
and fly off into the world on some dark night as good as anyone
else. Cook! You heard me.

LADY DUKE:
Listen to that naughty Clarie. Poor Cook, to be left in charge
of them! And yet, in fact, "fly off into the world on some dark
night" is just what they did. An epic journey – a six weeks'

tour that lasted years, through a part of France, Switzerland, Germany, and Holland. Let us now bring the fire in Cook's large stone fireplace out into the open, like so, and here let it become their campfire where we find them, on the bank of the famous Rhine.

The fire in the huge ancient fireplace moves out into the open and becomes a campfire.

Maery's face appears in its glow, while everything and everyone else fades away.

She clutches her Box Desk.

LADY DUKE:
Ah, now. Why, here she is – our Maery. Her face appears in its glow … contemplating – in a fleeting moment of solitude – its primal, elemental power.

The Witnesses read the following testimonies and then pass them along to Maery, who hesitates, not knowing what to do with them, and then puts them in the slot of her Box Desk. She does so with the blankness of one who has sealed her fate without knowing it.

WITNESS 1: It is important to note they were camping at the location the night before and were cooking on an open fire ring.

WITNESS 2: we stopped at a store got some hotdogs and rolls and a gallon of water then headed to the camp site. it was about 10pm when we got to the camp site and i think we took spot 19.

WITNESS 1: After the fire works we went back to my cousins place behind her house to camp out in the woods for the night. It was probably around 12:00 or 1 am when we had started to set camp up.

WITNESS 2: bout a month ago i was with a friend and her son, we were hanging out at a camp ground. i think the camp ground was part of by Allamuchy state park, either way it was on the Musconetcong river.

WITNESS 1: my friend was asleep, and i was lying next to the fire just listening to the sounds of the woods and river.

WITNESS 2: Anyhow we were basically in the middle of nowhere, on a 9 day camping trip with a Chevy pickup and a camper on the back. I went out one night to chip ice off the side of the river for our drinks and had an eerie feeling of being watched – I quickly ran back to our camper.

WITNESS 1: I had this weird feeling that there was something over to the right watching us, so I used my binoculars to scan the tree line.

We hear strains of the next song,
"I Never Slept."

But more creepy than sad.

4. TALES FROM THE CAMPINGPLATZ –
OPENING REMARKS

Here is a moment of creative conception: an outer mystery meets the recollection of an early, inner uncertainty.

ᔆ SONG: I NEVER SLEPT ᔆ

MAERY:
(*Sings*)
I never slept as a little girl.
I never slept as a little girl.
I'd be awake sometimes all night until just before dawn

(*Speaks*)
... when it was time to get up. I'd go to school exhausted
and my hair a mess. Clarie wasn't born yet and I didn't know
Fanny then. I was on the ground floor. Everyone else
was upstairs.

LADY DUKE:
(*Stage whispering with abandon, from the Lecture Hall after-hours*)
Ah-ha yes. We've arrived at GOTHICK: the 19th century with a
K on the end, redolent of the Dark Ages, portentously gloomy
or horrifying, yet darkly romantic all the same.

MAERY:
I heard something – walking around on the ground right outside my window. RIGHT outside! I was alone down there in the room where I was supposed to sleep,

(*Sings*)
and it was something big outside. On two feet. I'd hear it and I'd feel it.

(*Speaks*)
The hair on the back of my neck stood up.

LADY DUKE:
Indeed: all around us are footsteps, do you hear them? Something is circling the campsite – something bipedal and very, very large.

MAERY:
Once it started making noises.

(*Sings*)
That was the worst, um, night of all. That was the worst, yeah, night of all.

(*Speaks*)
Like some kind of banging that sounded like it was inside that tore my heart out of my little chest.

(*Sings*)
I don't know how I made it through.

(*Speaks*)
Once or twice before that I'd tried going upstairs to try and get them to help me. But when I stood at the door I could hear my dad was asleep, snoring, and that my stepmother wasn't.

That she lay there, awake, not sleeping and also not offering help or greeting – nothing could be scarier than that.

LADY DUKE:
(*In a loud, falsely confidential stage whisper*)
The "Second Mrs. Godwin"—

MAERY:
If I could go back now I would have called out, "I need my dad!" but I didn't know that language then. I didn't know what to do. I started to get cold. I was afraid of something that they didn't believe existed.

LADY DUKE:
(*Over at the window blind, looking out*)
I feel something – something is out there!

MAERY:
And yet it lurks in the darkness, just outside the reach of the lanterns, the campfire, in the dreams that signal a life beyond Life, in the shadows where the glaring laboratory lights of objectivity cannot reach. Waiting for me out there. Bigger than human and on two feet.

LADY DUKE:
(*As before, wildly listening*)
Wind through the boughs of large trees. Then the sounds of a large creature – watching us?

MAERY:
(*Sings*)
I stood there and stood there.

LADY DUKE:
What is the time on the little electric clock??

MAERY:

I was sure that she saw me there, that she was watching me through the dark.

I was too ashamed and petrified to reach out into the room with my voice. I knew only how to apologize, and even that always came out wrong.

LADY DUKE:
(*Feeling around, unable to see*)
So dark! As if a veil covers one's vision, in all directions ...

MAERY:

There was no curling up near the doorway, waiting and hoping to be found. I stood in the threshold of a most destructive waking nightmare that would haunt my every step toward the future. After a long time of knowing there was no friend or help, I turned away.

LADY DUKE:
(*Growing vaguely desperate*)
How many more hours until the sun begins to come back up again!? And will those hours pass quickly or slowly!!??

MAERY:
And so, in great fear and pain that I could not separate enough to identify ...

LADY DUKE:
So slowly the hours are dragging by ...

The Monster appears, in silhouette, among the dark trees.

MAERY:
I turned from that threshold,
I entered the world.

A membrane that separated me from the ordinary and safe
human world grew more opaque.
I stepped down very far
on the staircase.
I stepped much farther
than just downstairs – I kept stepping.
Past the cellar.
I began to go underground ...
Very, very far down, and never sought help again.

I later came to realize that the big creature walking around
outside my window was also living inside ... of ... me. And that
I'd truly never escape.

*The Witnesses read the following Testimonies and then pass them
to Maery, who is only hearing them with her Second Attention,
and who puts each one through the slot and into her Box Desk
without a fully realized or grounded consciousness of what
she's doing.*

WITNESS 1: The whole time walking back I had an uneasy
feeling like I was being watched.

WITNESS 2: I truly believe that when up there we were being
watched all the time.

LB:
(*As a disembodied voice outside of the circle of firelight*)
Who will care to tell a ghoulish tale?

MAERY:
(*In a dreamily baleful state, to no one in particular*)
I would.
Why shouldn't I ...

*Fond applause as LB appears, not only in firelight, but in
a spotlight.*

MAERY:
(*Startled*)
LB!

*Poet LB. With the turban and everything. Supremely foppish, lace
cuffs and lording it over everybody.*

LB:
Where were you, Maery?

MAERY:
Oh.

LB:
Do you not but enjoy to be here at the Campingplatz?

MAERY:
I do.

LB:
Here at the little bend in the river, where the teams would pull
the barges along back in the days ... South upstream ... North
downstream ... one of those rivers.

MAERY:
Yes, isn't it. Significant. And ...

LB:
 ... wide skirts, arrayed kerchiefs dabbed here, then there ...
wine country more and more the farther south ...

MAERY:
So lovely. And. And yet ...

LB:
(*Looking up to the dark hills*)
And yet.

MAERY:
When night falls ...

LB:
When night falls. There seems to be ...

MAERY:
Something else.

LB:
Doesn't there.

MAERY:
Indeed. And it watches us ... waiting to be remembered ....
Or imagined ...

They look up, scanning the imposing countenance of the dark hills above them. The Monster appears in silhouette, behind them. They are looking the other way.

LB:
Who were they, do you think, Maery? Those who came before—

MAERY:
(*Cont'd*)
To find out who they really were,
One will have to climb up and visit their holy grounds,
their groves,
and sit there for a long time,
and not knock anything down, and not build anything,
and sleep there,
surrounded by the wild boar herd, the swarms of bees in

odd places,
and gradually begin to intuit them, the fierce ancient people
who worshipped the stern works of Nature as unseparate from
their own bodily unfolding,
imagine their thoughts, and what they did.

*Again Witness 2 reads out some testimonies and hands them
to Maery, who absently inserts them into her Box Desk, which
remains fastened to her front.*

WITNESS 2: I truly believe that when up there we were being
watched all the time.

LB:
How do you feel?

MAERY:
(*Suddenly nauseous, caressing the Box Desk*)
Slightly pregnant.

LB:
Alright then I'll start.

Strains from "The Wild Nite Pigs" lead us into ...

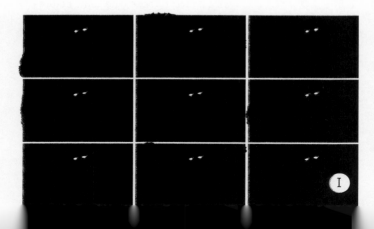

I

5. TALES FROM THE CAMPINGPLATZ –
MAERY THE GERMANIC GOTH

Dropping into another format of existence ...

LB:
(*Putting a hand over hers*)
I feel that you had an existence with them, Maery. Yes, and that you are taking a cue from these hills and crrrrrags that tower above this below, this, what had been to them a sacred River, now pulling us irrevocably to the place where they wait for us to join them. From its darkest and deepest recesses of the surrounding forest you are called back there, to assume control once again ...

THE WILD NITE PIGS (THE TUNE)

PEASANT MAIDS CHORUS:
The cliffs, the bluffs, the twisty footroutes, steep and punishing
Cliffs, the bluffs, the twisty footroutes, steep and punishing
Cliffs, the bluffs, the twisty footroutes ...

LB:
(*In place of Chorus lyrics*)
And this one's about YOU, Maery! Child Bride!
I imagine something? Or remember it?

Either way – it is site-specific.
Here is where we learn! About the Maery no one ever –
the Maery of No One! Never!
We sat on the bank, your skirts all arrayed,
and the ground itself went under change.

MAERY:
Something gurgling underneath?

The music trails off ...

LB:
Why, YE-ES, how did you gue-ess?
Darkly forested hills rise up before us, blocking the view.
A sunny wind was terrorizing your curls and at the same time
we uncannily observed a head of Medusa and a huge serpent
pass by, lolling and bobbing along the swift currents.

MAERY:
"Good-bye, Harriet! Goodbye, Hélène!"

LB:
You called out strangely. And waved to them.

LADY DUKE:
(Appearing in a camping outfit with equipment)
For those of you just joining us - Harriet was Percy Shelley's
wife, who eventually could not take anymore and took her own
life by drowning. Hélène was Cixous, the great, second wave,
mother of Post-Structural Feminist thought who wrote "Laugh
of the Medusa" – commanding all women to write their bodies.

MAERY:
(Feeling her body with her mind)
OH YEAAAAAHHHHH ...

LB:
(*Still rapt in the focus of the story*)
You had described around that same time awakening to
satanic forces in your attic rooms late at night // even though
you could see the garden from your windows, and so took to
sleeping out-of-doors instead, wrapped in deer hides (it's a
boring image in the end), with a pack of tamed dogs.

MAERY:
// "I perceive thee, Satan for I could not conjure thee in my
own imagination. I cannot form your image – "

LB:
And then you replied

MAERY:
"I begin to think I will rule this country."

LB:
And then a few years later, didn't you just …

From the Lecture Hall:

LADY DUKE:
LB is suggesting here that Maery reach back very far, at least
as far as *4ᵗʰ to 6ᵗʰ centuries AD or CE whatever you like – to
the time of the earliest manuscript evidence of the fierce and
ferocious tribes of the VisiGoths, OstroGoths -*
It seems there is a version of her, from that time … the time of
the *Goths, and their extinct Eastern Germanic Language. And
stretching back, of course, into late antiquity …*

LB:
(*Cont'd*)
There were few places that welcomed the dogs, for they killed
the flocks of ducks // and rabbits which you would then have

to gut and pluck and build huge fires on which to cook them so their bodies wouldn't go to waste as discarded carrion upon the banks.

MAERY:
(*Cheering on the dogs*)
// Yeah! Yeah! Yeah! Yeah! Yeah! // Yeah! Yeah! Yeah!

LB:
//Maery? Maery!

LB:
A barge called "Richard V" went by one day, from another realm of regional history, pulled along from the shore by a team of stout draft horses – that was how they did it then – and you were ready for them!

Maery S. steps out in Queenly VisiGoth Warrior Goddess battle gear and screams at the barge in Old Gothic, slashes the straps of her Box Desk (which drops to the ground and cracks) with a dagger and then pulls out her musket, aims, and fires.

BANG! BANG! .... BANG!

LADY DUKE:
How did she smuggle a MUSKET into this what time period is this ...?!

LB:
She shot his horses!!

MAERY:
(*Shouting*)
You there! Butcher them for curing into Rheinisches sauerbraten, traditionally made with horse meat, am I right? Tonight we feast on the banks!

CROWDS OF FOLK, AND LB:
Huh-YAH!!!!

LB:
The local Rhinelander folk, already enamoured with your roast
duck and hasenpfeffer stuffed with fruits and tender river
grasses, come to love you more and more.

MAERY:
Yeah, yeah yeah yeah yeah yeah yeah yeaaaaah! Eat up.

Lights fade on the riverbank scene.

LB:
These were stories. Murmurs over generations, of unspeakable
things that transpired in the hills above the river.
Collective memory –

LADY DUKE:
(*Patting the Box Desk, which she retrieves from the ground, with a
smug, wry smile*)
And collected. Memory.

LB:
– embedded in a geography.
The birds who nested out of the reach of the dogs would cry
and call them out, flying by over the water – the swans, the
diving birds, later the steam train carriages that rumbled by
carrying great ceramic pots, and logs.
Even far away, the craftsmen potters who grappled with
or worked to appease the malevolent ancient spirits who
plagued them – e'en they had heard of you, and the malevolent
Daemones Ceramici admired your fearlessness.

MAERY:

For I, too, pleasure in the smashing of the great ceramic vessels carried on the barges and trains. Feast after feast I serve to the goodly and gullible folk, and then tying myself to the tracks I derail the trains – rush its carriages and its flat cargo beds, slashing the binds and

smashing,

shattering,

crashing,

crushing.

Ha ha ha ha HAAAAAH! I AM SHE WHO WORKS HER WILL.

Maery S. is seen laughing daemonically and hypothetically participating in the pleasures of destruction with the Daemones Ceramici in their high, high land of salt and char.

LB:

(*Stepping back to survey her early work*)
Her early work ... puf puf puf ...

LADY DUKE:

(*Critically, curatorially*)
There's very much energy in it, it does lack focus. Its critique still feels scattered, and wants for consolidation of power ...

LB & MAERY:
We'll see ...

LADY DUKE:
Yes we shall ...

MAERY:
BLAEGHH!

X

LADY DUKE:
(Seeing the formal aspects at work)
One might give pause and ask here at this point: do Goths like metal? And certainly, one would be well within one's rights to ask. We are on the left bank of the Middle Rhine at the tail end of the Iron Age, after all, and so the quick answer is, yes they certainly did. And furthermore, Maery's present demeanor here does seem to signal a certain ***fusion genre known as Goth Metal, originating in the early 1990s, combining the heaviness of heavy metal with the dark atmospheres of gothic rock. Originally an outgrowth of death-doom, which itself was a fusion of death metal and doom metal. Prominent pioneers of gothic metal include Paradise Lost, My Dying Bride, and Anathema from Northern England, Type O Negative from the U.S., The Gathering from the Netherlands, and Theatre of Tragedy from Norway: a band which developed the 'beauty and the beast' vocal aesthetic of combining aggressive male vocals with clean female vocals[19], a contrast Maery embodies here with and within the whole of her being.***

LB:
It takes a long time for this image to fade. They who saw it with their own eyes admit that it was so seared into their minds and memories that it would be only a very long time after they themselves lay silent and committed to their graves that the image of Maery S. could be remade into that as a gentle, brilliant, if wayward, girl.
These stern branches and heavy old boughs that tower over us now from the cliffs overlooking this great and mighty river. They weren't even saplings yet, in a virgin forest at that time and it was their great-grandparents that witnessed it. Saw your deeds. Long ago. When the Germans were, instead: Germanics.

19. For those who would like to know more, it seems that the Lady Duke has obtained her definition of this cultural phenomenon from this link: https://en.wikipedia.org/wiki/Gothic_metal

... Germanics ...

Music loop. Everyone looks to the dark, imposing hills above the river.

LB:
(*Again stepping back*)
Several years later I learned about Harriet, Maery's unwitting rival, who had drowned herself in the Serpentine, and of Hélène, who would transmit the echo of the Medusa's laugh to all the world many long years after our death. My blood ran cold at the reckoning.
Puf puf puf.

MAERY:
And who was the real Medusa? Didn't you ever know? Ha ha the truth is so often concealed. She was not a monster. She was made into one because she was not white and refused to submit to conquering. Because she humiliated Alexander the Great at the first cataract, at the confluence of the Blue and the White Nile, when he came to take her land. She was not Greek. She was a Nubian Warrior Goddess, Kandake, or Candace – Amanirenas - with locks such as he had never seen. She wore a battle mask. It deified her, and without metaphor. She was one of a trinity, representing the truth and transformation that lay in both creation and destruction. In short: female wisdom. (Along with her sisters: Strength and Universality.)
Which, of course, poor fellow, he wanted no part of.
Alexander was afraid – the sight of her, flanked by all her army, sitting on her throne atop two elephants who held, served, and fought for her of their own will, was more than he could bear, and sent him packing. He and his "great" big army retreated back into Egypt. To hide his humiliation, he buried her truth in a false story of monstrousness.[20]

20. A debt is owed to the "United States of Africa" group page on Facebook for this explication.

6. TALES FROM the CAMPINGPLATZ –
A SCREAMING from the DARK HILLS above the RIVER

LADY DUKE:
(Frayed and breathless from the adventurous excursion, now speaking safely from the Lecture Hall, producing the exact page in the history books for proof)
Ah yes, here it is:

> **GOTH – a member of a Germanic people that overran the Roman Empire in the early centuries of the Christian era. Their peoples, their civilization, or their language, being characterized from the Western perspective as outlandish, rude, or brutal.[21] Foreign. Non-Hellenic. "Barbarian."**

All along the Rhine, for a long time, the Romans occupied the left bank, and the Tencteri, Usipetes, Menapii, Eburones tribes occupied the right. Later on, in the 5th century, the Alemanni and the Franks would drive the Romans out altogether, setting up their own cities. It is this side – which remains the most civilized to this day – where Maery and LB now sit, conjuring up ancient stories through the portal of their campfire.

---

21. Definition adapted from Nick Groom's "The Gothic: A Very Short Introduction." Oxford University Press, 2012.

MAERY:
(*Panting. Re: "Barbarians"*)
HAH!
(*To LB*)
LB.

LB:
Yes, Maery?

MAERY:
That was a really good story.

LB:
Yes. Yes it was. Well done. Puf puf puf...

MAERY:
To have Worked My Will!

LB:
Maery, Maery. Why cannot you see. That you are she.

He hands her a bouquet of strange, dark, and faded flowers. They creep and spread into flowering vines everywhere, a delirium of flowers in which one might easily drown, during the following.

MAERY:
(*Stepping forward now, looking up to the dark hills from her area of the bank*)
There is a secret up there isn't there. In those darkly wooded hills above the river. Something very old.

LB:
Yes, Maery? Yes. There is seeing and there is sensing.
Something watches us. We are in the presence of something.

Maery looks up at the dark hills and cliffs, animating a frightful scene with her words.

*Her panting slows as her breath gathers meaning, her hands
searching her own torso, she sings.*

∾ SONG: WHATE'ER GURGLED ∾

What e'er gurgled 'neath the ground
by my mother's grave has craped its way

(*Speaking*)
up the rock face and now lurks in those hills. Something
we will never see written in history, only for a moment in a
lifetime, passing in the shadows.

(*Singing*)
What phantasmal womb can travel over time

(*Speaking*)
and landscape? Turned unnaturally in on itself –

(*Singing*)
what collapsed / corroding mother?

(*Speaking*)
And what is the thing that it carries and wants to put forth?

(*Singing*)
Something we can only know by awe, and gnawing fear.

LB:
Ahem. Well.

WITNESS 1: She said she believed her husband because he does
not scare easily and his face was white when he came back
into camp to tell her of the encounter.

MAERY:
Where's Percy? Where's Clarie.

LB steps forward puffing slowly at his pipe, also looking up at the hills.

LADY DUKE:
For those of you just joining us: our Maery, her sister Clarie, and the famed Romantic poet Percy Shelley, yes yes yes, with whom she had already been cavorting on the grave of her mother, in the St. Pancras Cemetery, and here we are, with this even more famous poet, this "LB" – have a guess, will you? That incorrigible scoundrel, supremely foppish lace cuffs and always game for churning up trouble with other people. Meanwhile, the search party never came for the girls and they immersed themselves more deeply in intensity, hinkiness and hanky panky before vista after opening vista. This was the era of vastness, pleasure, and possibility for them, and well-nigh the only that they would get, for many problems would plague them later ...

Maery stands in the open.

MAERY:
(*Aside*)
Indeed. So many ghoulish tales. And all making direct reference to what would come.
This field in which we stand, not far from the banks of the Northward-flowing river, is a stand-in for a place within my heart.
When I eloped with Percy abroad, the ghoulishness was only just hanging about in the tales that we told.
No matter where I roam, across ranges and through ages, I return here to it.
When I am ready to give birth but then don't.

When the money runs out.
When the child is born, but can't stay, and doesn't live.
When I learn to ask for help, and to say thank you, I return here to become. Again, again, and again to hasten the birth of my self. I come back here. I come here again. Repeating, repeating, repeating. To confirm my own mysteries. To retreat beneath my most private veil. An endless returning. I bring into further hiding the triple presence of my one life's deeply layered events. Here, I foretell it: all that I will have to face, and all the failures I will have to make, until I find what and who it is that I am to embody.
(Turning South, in full connection with the source of her power)
I turn to the South.

Lightning strikes.

At the crossroads of the path is seen the imposing outline of a massive, frightening figure.

MAERY:
(Speaking with some alternate level of attention than that of the action of the play, to the figure)
And to encounter you, at the crossroads.

Deep rumbles of thunder (from some insane, olden outdoor subwoofer) follow the flashes, which reveal the swift retreat of the figure towards the South Woods.

WITNESS 1: About 3/4 of the way home something came off the side of the road and followed me so fast and so close I had no distance enough to brake.

WITNESS 2: I started to turn my head to the left and got as far as the passengers front fender and my hair stood straight up. My eyes were watering like crazy, hands were sweaty

WITNESS 1: Can't recall any landmarks, was in shock afterwards, so my mind is a blank after it happened. Don't even know how we made it home, we were shaking so much.

WITNESS 2: I turned more to my left to see something standing in the middle of the road.

When the inexplicable figure is gone, Maery turns to the gathered, returning, and returned audience.

MAERY:
Ah, there's Clarie. Clarie after all.

OBSCENE SUBSCENE:
CAMPINGPLATZ HOOK-UP: LB + CLARIE.

From the opposite angle Clarie comes bounding into the light spilling from the campfire and spills herself all over LB.

MAERY:
At that moment Clarie came bounding back in, with very rosy cheeks. She humprushed LB, latched on to his leg, didn't stop humping at it for the remainder of the scene. Gently at first and then not-so-gently.
"Hullo ... Handsome ... I don't believe we've met. I am unmarried Clarie. I love your lips. I remember you and your pants. I like the way you talk. I'm a big fan ...." Etc. etc. etc.
(*As Clarie*)
Hump, hump. Hump.
(*As herself*)
Where's Percy?

But Clarie was too busy humping to even hear the question.

LB:
We're telling ghoulish tales.

MAERY:
That was an "ENCHANTING!" idea to Clarie and then she
decided she was "SCARED of how DARK" it was and that
made the humping more aggressive.
Clarie was tired of everyone else going in the churchyard, and
here was this "SO GORGEOUS GUY" who could do the job
just fine –
(*Sighing*)
Her grasping of him was embarrassing for everyone else.
(*As Clarie*)
Hump, hump.

Journal of Maery S. Page 38.
Season of Crickets and Goldenrod, 1814.

My poor, dear stepsister Clarie who is as much sister
to me as any could be – I've chosen not to notice
whether or not Percy'd turned his attentions onto her
– daughter-of-a-free-thinker such as I am. And now
that LB has joined us she's dropped the idea of winning
Percy like a hot potato. She appears ready to spend the
fullness of her natural luxuriance on a one-fortnight-
stand with the most infamous of irresponsible narcissists,
who – disastrously – also happens to be a lot of fun.

MAERY:
(*Cont'd*)
She was in his presence two weeks, when he was feeling bored,
// and he had her with child....

LB:
// I'm feeling bored *now*.

MAERY:
(*As Clarie*)
Hump.
(*Cont'd as herself*)
Claire latched on, she felt she had no choice, she couldn't think
about anything else //, she wanted to do it again and again, and
LB had other interests -
(*As Clarie*)
Hump, hump.

LB:
(*Becoming Cook somehow for a split second, who shakes her head*)
// You girls ...

MAERY:
(*As Clarie*)
Hump.

LB:
(*As himself*)
Can't you see I'm busy. It's time for me to start my crafts.

MAERY:
(*Making crafts*)
Don't reject her, LB, you'll only make her worse.
(*As Clarie*)
"Shuh-tup, MAEry." *Hump.*

LB:

Paper plates anyone? Pot of paste? Googly eyes? // Popsicle sticks? Pipe-cleaners in prim'ry coleurs?

MAERY:

// Sure I'll take some googly eyes ...
Meanwhile, Clarie, spent but still eager:
"Let's do it again!"

MAERY / LB:
Whew! / Ugh.

LB:

Ahem. Well.
Suddenly big bundles electrical connections.
Now satellite dishes, zipper-up porches, toaster ovens ... all the comforts of home ... flower pots.

MAERY:

The future always found us so quickly.
(*As Clarie*)
Hump.

LB:

Then on to the next camplingplatz – Sonnenstrand ... Loreley ...
We see the arrival of electricity ... //
Connection cables lying laid along the ground, connecting supply box supplying megawatts power to each of the plätze ...

MAERY:
(*Approaching and fingering some cables*)
Hmm. Electricity. Hmmm ....

WITNESS 1: Our group became quite nervous so we lit a fire and kept a close watch at the mentioned area. About 30 mins later we heard a repetative grunting sound some distance away. Needless to say, we did not investigate the area as most of our group was quite terrified and we cautiously left several min later.

WITNESS 2: We were camping in late spring 1983 near Mills Creek.

WITNESS 1: everybody in the campground had gone to bed. No fires, no lights from RV's, no noise but this screaming.

LB:
Dear God, who is screaming like that??? Who screams amid our idyll, in some language inaccessible to the average European – what is it!? – is it Welsh? Japanese?

WITNESS 1: We all heard it. It was confusing to us because no known language was discernible.

WITNESS 2: There were definite patterns and cadence similar to hearing someone speak a language that you are not familiar with. You can hear words and the sounds seem to be slurred into one another. just the high decibel level ... that was vocal and trying to say something to me.

LB:
Ahem. Having concluded this chapter of the presentation, I shall now stalk moodily off into the woods, counter-intuitively toward that terrible screaming.

LB fastens a very old piece of paper to the trunk of a tree.

The sounds of the forest, the swamp, the mountains all die away.
Only the scream remains, until it spends itself into a terrible, low
moan, groans, turns mournful, and dies out.

MAERY:
(With growing alarm and worry)
Where is Percy? No, really ...

Clarie gets preggers, LB flees the scene, leaving only a series of
notes nailed to some trees leading us along a treacherous pathway.

The first one reads:

You must needs be prevented from following me
I speak to you from the miraculously bleak future.
What sacred ritual ground of antiquity
Is now gravel parking lot across the street from
the krankenhaus? Still more deeply into the
shadows of steep mountain forests.
Ghosts caper in costume of early region, regional
specialty now long forgotten.
Think of it as a guided hike, without the guide.
Though time and civilization have advanced as far
as they have,
One must nonetheless still beware:
The Wild Night Pigs.

7. TALES FROM THE CAMPINGPLATZ –
THE WILD NIGHT PIGS

The series of notes that LB leaves behind lead to some disturbing yet darkly inspiring scenes enacted by regional ghosts upon crumbling structures in the hills.

We hear some strange grunting, rummaging, and foraging in the leaf litter on the ground.

We come to a large bonfire and gather round. The ghosts of the Peasant Maids appear upon crumbling structures of stacked stones, and sing a welcome song.

SONG: WILD NIGHT PIGS

PEASANT MAIDS CHORUS:
(Singing, aggressively)
The cliffs, the bluffs, the twisty footroutes, steep and punishing
Cliffs, the bluffs, the twisty footroutes, steep and punishing

REGIONAL GHOST HOST:
(Shouting, lasciviously)
NOTHING WRITTEN ABOUT ANY SERVANT,
BUT PLENTY ABOUT MULE TRAVEL THROUGH
THE MOUNTAINS!

PEASANT MAIDS CHORUS:
The cliffs, the bluffs, the twisty footroutes
The Wild Night Pigs!

REGIONAL GHOST HOST:
FOLLOW, PURSUE, COME AFTER, SNARE!

PEASANT MAIDS CHORUS:
The Wild Night Pigs!

REGIONAL GHOST HOST:
BECOME, OCCUR, COME, PASS!

PEASANT MAIDS CHORUS:
The Wild Night Pigs!

REGIONAL GHOST HOST:
CHOOSE, TEST, THE CATASTROPHE!

PEASANT MAIDS CHORUS:
The Wild Night Pigs!

REGIONAL GHOST HOST:
OF LIFE FORCE RE-ENTERING LONG-LIFELESS FLESH!

PEASANT MAIDS CHORUS:
The Wild Night Pigs!

REGIONAL GHOST HOST:
(*Shouting*)
AFTER IT'S FORMED, NOT ALONGSIDE!

PEASANT MAIDS CHORUS:
The Wild Night Pigs!

REGIONAL GHOST HOST:
WRONG-DOING, SIN!

PEASANT MAIDS CHORUS:
The cliffs, the bluffs, the twisty footroutes, steep and punishing
Cliffs, the bluffs, the twisty footroutes, steep and punishing

REGIONAL GHOST HOST:
NOTHING WRITTEN ABOUT ANY SERVANT,
BUT PLENTY ABOUT MULE TRAVEL THROUGH
THE MOUNTAINS!

PEASANT MAIDS CHORUS:
The cliffs, the bluffs, the twisty footroutes
The Wild Night Pigs!

REGIONAL GHOST HOST:
SEIZE, GRASP, COVETOUSNESS!

REGIONAL GHOST HOST:
MONEY-BOX, CHEST!

PEASANT MAIDS CHORUS:
The Wild Night Pigs!

REGIONAL GHOST HOST:
LIBERATE, SET FREE, LEAVE, PERMIT!

REGIONAL GHOST HOST:
SWINE, PIG, DOOR, BE FULL!

PEASANT MAIDS CHORUS:
The Wild Night Pigs!

REGIONAL GHOST HOST:
MADE OF DIRT, GODLESS, UNHOLY!

PEASANT MAIDS CHORUS:
The Wild Night Pigs!

REGIONAL GHOST HOST:
PROFANE, SPEAK, ENTANGLE!

PEASANT MAIDS CHORUS:
The Wild Night Pigs!

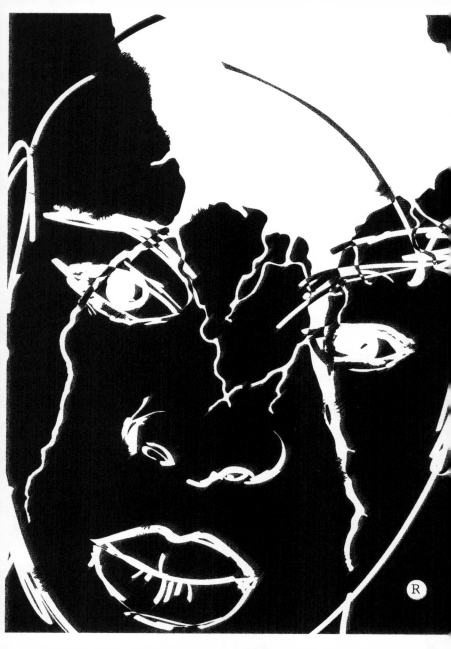

 HEAPING OF CONSEQUENCE

Then lo! at dawn's dim, earliest beam began
Beneath their feet a groaning of the ground:
The wooded hill-tops shook, and, as it seemed,
She-hounds of hell howled viewless through the shade,
To hail their Queen.

For now she would arrive.

- The Aeneid

7.5. TALES FROM THE CAMPINGPLATZ –
VALE OF SATAN

The two fetching Peasant Maids step forth in unison. As if to answer the objection, answer to the objectification. They speak in a popcorn-stitch fashion.

RIGHT AND LEFT PEASANT MAIDS:
(*In unison*)
And now I will tell you a tale.

One day, as we young maidens were strolling along, and the windy breeze caught up with the sun in our wild windy curls and braids with flowers and vines plaited in, we saw something large and fast and very dark swing up over the ridge of the gorge. (It was Satan.) We saw the thing before we heard it. Lingering suspended aloft for one moment, spread black wings, and then took a lightning bolt's fall toward the river. When we did hear, we were deafened by the screaming roar of sound. It tore through the sky and humbled the land. That sound – if that's not too inadequate a term (it was more of an event than a sound) was a great mouth opening sideways, and consuming everything unto itself. The thing dropped straight down toward the river, pulled up again, careened arrogantly around sharp bends through the twists of the cliffs above the banks, then thrust with unthinkable power upward again – catapulting itself over the rim of the escarpments and pulling into great distances with terrible force to some otherwhere. The fear and hatred it had instantly put into our hearts – hardly significant to its self – whereas we had been altered forever.

The step of a dance, so nicely.

We never just walked about in the open after that, but learned always to seek cover instead – of trees, of buildings. Long porticos were erected. In nearby Oberwesel the cow-herdsmen's stone-pile passageways and the watchmen's towers were restored and put back into use almost immediately, and nobody said a word as to why make those heavy efforts. Except the children, who were quietened up quickly, and reminded the difference between a devil and Satan.

A promenade of wistful lost dreams. The music becomes a lament.

You can now stroll through them as at leisure, wander through their overhanging arches, their overarching columns, for pleasure. We instinctively built them to speak to nature's beauty. You don't know what they are or why they are there, and you feel protected, though you know not from what.

We just told you what. Hopefully you were listening.

They reach the conclusion, the resolution of the woven steps of the promenade they have made. Their feet itch. Yet they attempt to issue a warning.

When you go, though. Know that in Oberwesel you will see few people, and no faces. It's as if the faces of people have been sanded off and are now useless as an identifying mark. As if the terrible sound of that day had burned away the features of the people of the region. But they are good at hiding it – with a bonnet, a long wide sleeve held just so, or a turning of the other cheek. They don't assault you with their affliction.

Then the ghosts are gone. We find: Another note! Maery reads all of the notes aloud, and is accompanied by LB's voice at the same time.

What happened here?
In the wooded gorge below
Digging up a body or disposing of the remains of a body. Most likely one very large body.
And then a storm rolls in, and lightning strikes.

MAERY:
(Absently thumbing through some Witness testimonies from a stack she has collected and not inserted yet into her Box)
Hmmm ... such girlishness ... Such ghoulishness ... dark secret watching from the hills ... hmmm ...
Something feels as if to be forming ...

LB:
(Suddenly popping out from behind a tree)
Does it REALLY????

Sudden, fond applause. He tacks another note to a tree, then completely disappears, for good. Lightning strikes.

And may it serve as a reminder:
Just when you start getting used to the rummaging of the Night Pigs that gather in herds about your tent, you begin to hear something else ...

WITNESS 2: I will never forget that. It makes the hair on my neck stand on end to this day.

A heavier step on the leaves and fallen branches...

MAERY:
(*Cont'd*)
... One very large body .... Lightning strikes ... (the harnessing of electricity into cables like arms & legs) ...
Plates left out overnight are re-arranged in the morn, with crushed songbirds on ...

The memory of the idyll is over.

LADY DUKE:
(*Caught taking a sip of premium afternoon tea*)
Ah and here we return to the version of our Maery, from Scene 4. All of the signs and signifiers point us to:

> **19th century, the Gothick with the K on the end, redolent of the Dark Ages, portentously gloomy or horrifying, yet darkly romantic all the same. It's the one where the young woman is running away from the ominous Victorian house in her nightgown ...**

WITNESS 1: It spooked the hell out of me so much so I have not camped since.

But then, there are sudden heavy bags and cases.

Maery is joined by Cook, who appears out of nowhere and reunites with her. They retrieve the lead of a small mule, named Smule, and seem to have no choice but to pick up everything and keep moving. Their plodding progress is traced along the MAPESTRY.

Just then, strange figures become visible, approaching from the treeline. Small, ghostly figures without faces.

LADY DUKE:
Or actually, I think I might say –

> **Gothic (of Literature): Of or relating to a style of fiction characterized by the use of desolate or remote settings and macabre, mysterious, or violent incidents.**

Indeed! Led by LB's notes and chased by the Wild Nite Pigs, the group crosses from the 'civilized' left bank that the Romans had conquered – however temporarily – to the side of the tribes. Forsaken by civilized society in retribution for their wanton transgressions against it, they crossed into those same dark hills at which they quaked only scant weeks and months or years ago.

By this point, you see, the children have been born but have mostly died in infancy, and so all of the toddlers in their entourage are ghosts.

The small, ghostly figures waft toward the group of travelers in procession, singing a haunting, and haunted, dirge. They are like wan puppets with a strange, eerie glow. Maery sits on one of the trunks and pens a quick journal entry which accompanies and explicates their song. Mrs. Wills fades out as the Ghosted Children arrive, singing, and pluck locks of their hair and place them in Maery's Box Desk as she writes, walking next to Smule and leaning her Box Desk on his already-piled-high-with-parcels-and-luggage back.

Journal of Maery S. Page 45.
Season of Cobwebs, Wind, and Empty Branches, 1814.

We are a group plodding along throughout the Europe. Minus Cook and all the cookeries and plus the ghosts of several infants, toddlers, and children: our broken branches, though we are but saplings and runners ourselves, trailing along with us, our first failed opportunities, the imprints of our treasures taken. And a small mule named Smule. We decided to send for Fanny this time as well, to avoid later unpleasantness. It is a plan which will ultimately also fail. She is already here, waiting for us, as we come suddenly indoors.

MAERY:
(*Increasingly fraught*)
Aw but it's a shoddy indoors, isn't it?

As Fanny put it, glumly,
"It's a rental."

*The party immediately resumes mule travel through the
mountains, in song. The MAPESTRY traces their progress through
the states of being/countries of Europe.*

 ## SONG TO GESTATE A MONSTER BY: "AND ONWARD UP"

Rhine, Rhine, Rhine
An inn, in the lakes region of Italy
And onward up, and onward up
Switzerland, Switzerland, Switzerland
And onward up, and onward up
Deutsche, Deutsche to Dutch
To Scotland
And onward up, and onward up
AND ONWARD UP, and onward up
And onward up, and onward up
AND ONWARD UP, and onward up
And onward up, and onward up
AND ONWARD

*Maery blindly and unquestionningly changes the diaper of a
ghost baby.*
*The rest of the crew files in with trunks and loads and bundles
and crowds about, wan, tired, and irritable.*

CLARIE:
(*Aside*)
When you imagine traveling through the mountains you only
see the sunny, blistering, bracing days. You don't see it with the
fogs. You don't smell the excrement of mules.

Journal of Maery S. Page 46.
Season of Black Flies, Roses,
and Lightning Storms, 1815.

I don't know if this is before or after my Percy and
Jane's husband were lost and drowned at sea. I don't see
Percy anywhere so perhaps a little of both. Everything
gets sort of jumbled together. If they're still alive then
they're somewhere lolling about in the boat, rifling and
rummaging through their ideals as men poets will do.
It's a big crowd, living and dead. The house and
accounts keeping have been left to me. And I'm not
very good at it.

The filmy figures of Percy and LB are seen through fog, at oars on
the glassy surface of the Lake. They converse in a language that is
made up strictly of the Great Ideas and nothing else.

MAERY:
Meanwhile, Fanny is like,
"WHAT *IS* THIS? WHERE ARE WE? WHERE HAVE
YOU BEEN??"

Journal of Maery S. Page 47.
Season of Damp Mists, Wet Leaves,
and Freezing Fogs, 1815.

It's winter. Dreariness, no more camping ... but
continued travel. We are given to restlessness.

MAERY:

Clarie ever looking for the next campingplatz, and the next,
and the next, sure that "the next one will be so lovely, won't
it? Just like on the Rhein – like it USED to be: lots and lots of
people, and sunshine, all lined up along at the riverbed in their
campers – do you remember!? They've got – I like the –
people camping –"
... Until she'd reached the limit of her imagination.
"Oh, That's as far as my imagination will go."

*A stack of letters arrives in the mail, immediately becoming
scattered. A voice issues from it.*

VOICE OF LB:

Allow me to see what I can do to pick up the thread.

MAERY:

A letter from LB in the scattered stack of mail. It was
addressed to me, but Clarie ripped it open. "Well, it's addressed
to Maery but. He's MY boyfriend!"

She tears it open as Clarie.

Letter from LB to Maery S.:

Keep hopping.
Some campers are more permanent.
You'll find these farther up into the hills.
Into the dark, dark hills on that foreboding,
anciently secretive Right Bank.

Ps: Please tell Claire I have inserted her child into a convent — school I think it's in Italy. I think it's probably fine. I'm sure. I'm sure the child is fine.

MAERY:
Clarie didn't realize she'd already been born ...
Then, leave it to Fanny to always find the Eviction notice in the stack. All right then, so we've got to pack up again and find another platz it looks like. Fanny! For fuck's sake! We've just got to *this* one!
(*As Fanny and Clarie, wincing and flinching at the sudden profanity of her language*)
Maery!!
(*Now as Maery again*)
So we follow with mules – well, Smule. We've got a small mule. Named Smule. And no mention of servants in the travel diaries.
Fanny is too depressed, and Clarie tries to throw as many fits as she can. That way she's .... "part of things," and she "can have some creativity to do too." If she wakes up and screams that "there are rats climbing all over" her face? "That's creativity. That's sucking in on the divine."

There wasn't much to be done with either Clarie or Fanny in any imaginable scenario.

Maery finds another stack of mail, the rest of it sent by creditors and by Harriet and it causes a row ...

MAERY:
It seems there is a stack of mail always following us.

Pleading and threats from Harriet, postcards sent by creditors, eviction notices – how I detest them! The bills find me but the not the checques.

Fanny had the nerve to suggest that morning that if "you can't afford this sort of lifestyle or you don't have the stomach for its consequences then you ought to go home. Or at the very least get direct deposit."

"Home to where, you foogy botch! YOU go home!"

"Home to Daddy," says Fanny, "He's probably wondering where you are by now." And then she called me a "sluuty kjunt!"

Here the row is building and is about to break.

(*As if to Fanny*)

Go back home! To where! To what!

At that, Clarie turned her head of ringlets toward us to tell us something.

"You know," she said, "I could have been played by Bernadette Peters at one time, you dutty clitches."

Uh-oh. Then she stands up.

"There's nothing wrong with me!" she shouts,

"Nothing wrong with me!

I just WANT!

Why is that so terrible?

I WANT!

Why can I never just be given WHAT I WANT!?"

And what can you say to that?

But it was then that Fanny stood up, screaming savagely,

(*as Fanny*)

"Where did you get that MONOLOGUE!!???"

Now the row breaks.

Truly hideous, gloriously ugly.

Squealing and screeching and struggling, careful curls flying and thrashing.

When it was over, I remember, many ringlets were frizzled. Dangling. And modifying.

9. PLATZ-HOPPING -
PRECESSION of the GHOSTED CHILDREN

Journal of Maery S. Page 49.
Season of Gray Ice and Gloom, 1816.

*And so we girls have arrived to a somewhat glum and
serious future, just as Cook had predicted in her rousing
number at the Skinner Street hearth: we find ourselves
utterly shunned by the stern society we scandalized
so gleefully at the outset. With the onset of winters,
careless platz–hopping and mountainous mule travel
become surreptitious RV squatting in overgrown and
empty campingplätze where retirees once lived on long–
term lease but have now abandoned in death.*

COOK:
(*Puffing on her pipe, indignantly*)
Cracking open some babushka dolls is what they're doing now
– a little less than halfway through - and getting more and
more unreasonable in shape all the time ...

Journal of Maery S. Page 49.
Mud season, 1816.

Our merry campfires have retreated to the past, and been replaced by a small propane camping cooker – single burner – over which Cook, who has again rejoined us, labors heavily and has retired from any and all musical performance at this point. Outside it rains glumly and gloomily, and seemingly permanently. Mould covers the walls of this abandoned camper in which we squat.

COOK:
They'll never get 'em back together. (*Puff puff puff*) Not now anyways. (*Puff puff puff*)

Journal of Maery S. Page 49.
Season of Soggy Soap, Mouse Poop, and Forget-Me-Nots, 1816.

All I know is that we're broke once again and if only it were another hundred and fifty or so years into the future, we'd all be addicted to methyl amphetamine and HP Lovecraft novels.

Our children have either been born dead or have died in infancy, and so all of the babies and toddlers in our entourage are ghosts. Any living ones (fathered by LB) were sent to the convent schools. We hope against hope that they are probably fine.

Journal of Maery S. Page 50.

 SONG: THE FIRST CHORUS
OF GHOSTED CHILDREN:

*Season of Musty Drywall,
Fruit Flies, and Bats, 1817.*

You often wake to listen
To the laboured breathing
Of all us lost children
You can't help it
We tell you not to torture
yourselves
Lying awake at night
List'ning to us struggle to
respire
We gather round your beds
Spectral and helpless
Before the repeating tide
Of sickness, tragedy,
and death

*We often awake to listen to the
laboured breathing of all our
lost children. We can't help it.
They tell us not to torture
ourselves, lying awake
at night, listening to them
struggle to respire.
They gather round our beds,
spectral and helpless before the
repeating tide of sickness and
tragedy and death...*

*Journal of Maery S. Page 50. Season of Sagging
Gutters and Crusty Fungus, 1817.*

I guess this is turning into a new ghoulish tale now ...

Another stack of mail arrives.

MAERY:
ANOTHER stack of mail!!?? I hope it's not more bad news ...

Letter from LB to Maery S.:
Bad news, Maery. (mumble mumble mumble)
You'll be the one to break it to Claire, won't
you? I DO wish there were something I
could do, but it was and is very important
that I not be bothered just now. I know you
understand. Xoxoxox LB

MAERY:

(*Aside*)

How is one to mother when one hasn't been mothered?
So we've lost another child to typhus fever.
To keep it from Claire, I'd have to pretend that nothing
happened, that her daughter was totally fine in the convent,
still alive, and not even sick. Typhus is always site specific. You
can see that it's going to happen when you visit the places.
The fact is it was badly placed in a kind of boggish area that
held a lot of wetness and didn't get a lot of wind. So it was only
a matter of time before infection and contagion found them
there. Cloudy morn. Foggy bog. Tops of the school buildings
in and out of visibility. Foogy bog. Foggy boog. Foogy-boog-
Boogie-man, Foogy booger. Ahem. This is a very sad story so I
don't - Booger. // Booger man. Wood booger. Excuse me. Wood-
boogie. Stump jumper. I beg your pardon. Two-egg boogie-
woogie stump-jumper. Anyhow, the mother, that being Clarie,
didn't think she had a choice about leaving her there until the
daughter was already dead – which is always the case.

FANNY:
// Maery?

MAERY:
(*Cont'd*)
And: then the whole thing opens up and one can see all kinds of other possibilities that at the time seemed impossibilities because of the seemingly insurmountable inconveniences. But later on when one realizes that the very life of your beloved young one was in question and at real risk, you would have done anything, overturned whole governmental structures and lived in penury, to get her away from there. For now she is gone and there is no getting her back is there? And now is the matter of breaking the bad news. I'm being very nice here ...

Music.

MAERY:
(*Cont'd*)
Claire, Clarie? Please come in here.

Clarie enters, twirling a ringlet about her fingers.

MAERY:
I hate to be the one to tell you this, but ...
(*Aside*)
I just remember the way she looked at me. As if willing the terrible news back into me.
She just kept saying, repeating over and over again, "No. No. No. No. No. No. No."

Everyone is sad.

Terribly sad
Terribly sad
Terribly sad
to lose a child,

(*Instrumental 4 bars*)

Terribly sad
Terribly sad
Terribly sad
to have to lie,

(*Instrumental 4 bars*)

Terribly sad
Terribly sad
Terribly sad
not to understand
each other and go
separate ways
though side by side
unto death.

(*Instrumental 4 bars*)

Terribly sad
Terr-ib-ly ... sad

Because of the dampness, the fire has completely gone out. A sad, thin plume of smoke ribbons its way up the chimney and the coals and ashes are black and wilted with moisture. Once outside, the plume of smoke partially solidifies and assumes the shapes of the

Chorus of Ghosted Children. They float around the house, and attend on Maery as she enters her reflections on the sad events in her journal, following along in song. As she writes, the Ghost of Clarie's now-deceased daughter wafts toward the spectral scene, and places her own lock of hair in Maery's Box Desk.

Journal of Maery S. Page 52.

SONG: THE SECOND
"CHORUS OF GHOSTED
CHILDREN":

Season of Spiders, Owls, and Dusty Rusts, 1818.

You know, you really should believe
That ghosts of all us children gather round,
In fact, all of your maternal disappointments
from day one, are trying to lead you to something.

You know, I cannot help but wonder, that the ghosts of all these children gathered round, in fact all of our maternal disappointments from day one, are trying to lead us to something.

MARY:
Way, way, way later, I was played by Natasha Richardson. When she died of a skiing accident, later that night, so did I. Again. The secret, fatal injury was only a de-manifestation coming to pass, the transformation death brings to matter. I saw, again, the thin Veil of life as I passed through it, of our beliefs that barely make up this whisper of a reality, through which we must cross back and forth over and over in one life, in many forms, up upon the mountain, on the hard packed snow, to an immaterial state.

WITNESS 1: At the end of the boardwalk I thought about going into the bog to look for it and fear of the unknown caused me to turn back.

WITNESS 2: Being in these openings felt strange so I would turn back and continue on the main trail.

WITNESS 1: NOBODY BUT ME. I HAVE ONLY TOLD A VERY FEW PEOPLE. I FELT AS IF I WAS BLESSED TO SEE SUCH A THING.

WITNESS 2: THE NAME OF OUR CLAIM WAS GRANDBABIES MINING CO. MY PARTERS NAME WAS CHARLES HASENBECK. HE IS DEAD NOW.

LADY DUKE:
Because I actually played and was Jane Williams in another version of my life (when you're as wealthy as I am you have access to several – so fortunate for me, I'm so grateful), the woman who was widowed along with Maery when their husbands died in a storm out at sea, I can now stand on tenterhooks with her, gazing apprehensively out at the vast horizon for signs of news, and remember it.

Maery and Jane are standing on tenterhooks looking apprehensively out at the horizon of the sea.

MAERY:
(*To the sea*)
Any news? Anything from out there on the horizon of the sea?

JANE:
No. No news.

Maery reaches out to comfort her and join in widowly sorrow by touching her on the shoulder.

MAERY:
If we're to be widows, then we'll be widows together, Jane.

But Jane evades the caress. She goes and whispers something to someone about Maery. Something that isn't nice. Something about her box of keepsakes, and how she's going to have it refurbished.

LADY DUKE:
And then, we come to:

10. BECOMING of a MONSTER

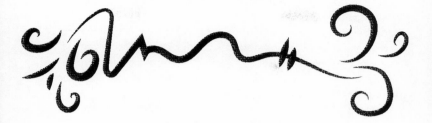

The GOTHIC NOIR: An interesting variant on film genre: set in the past, usually in Victorian England or America, yet with the settings of the modern city and its gallery of city characters. Shot in an Expressionist manner with deep shadows, and ornate art direction. The dangerous situations of the Gothic novel become the more extreme, doomed situations of the Noir film. A more actively engaged female protagonist, one seeking some kind of agency or control (even in a manner that is not exactly straightforward), emerges, realizes she has been under a thrilling but fatal spell, and pays the high price of the corruption of her soul, in an attempt to escape.[22]

MAERY:

(*Cont'd, now sheltering with her sisters in a dilapidated crate*) Meanwhile, my financial situation gets more and more disastrous. Percy couldn't leave us a red cent – it wasn't ever his own money to leave. My stupid mother (step-mother, actually) cashed a big fat chercque I had written her for the mortgage even though I SPECIFICALLY told her not to until she had heard from me that the coast was *clear* and the *cash* was in the *account*. So now even if the chercques I'm waiting

---

22. Definition adapted from Marc Svetov's "Noir and the Gothic" from his "Beyond the Fedora" series, Part One, in the Noir City Sentinel, Oct/Nov 2008.

for show up, I'm overdrawn by so much that they'll just get sucked into the vacuum of overdraft charges. Farggen klootch. We had enough food until I dropped the jar of my favorite pickles and it shattered everywhere. What a mess to clean up. And so no more pickles unless you want to risk eating broken glass. I've been using the same piece of dental floss for four or five days now and it's starting to fray. I now have to face up to the very real idea of mouthstink. It's fucking freezing outside. Yesterday I was reduced to stealing toilet paper from Moose and Sadies, and I got caught. I was like, 'HOW?' They were like, 'we saw you do it on the security camera' and I was like 'you SECURITY CAMERA'd ME IN THE **BATHROOM**???' Also: 'What is a security camera' and 'I want a lawyer!' But everyone knows I can't afford a lawyer. My agent isn't returning my phone calls or emails. We were arrested. Me, Clarie, Fanny. Fanny's used the jailing as a proper excuse and tried to hang herself from the pipes up by the ceiling of the jail cell but they broke with the weight and of course it turns out the pipes were toilet // plumbing pipes. Of corpse. Mrs. Wills is nowhere to be found. This ain't no campfire story anymore.

AUDIENCE PLANT:
// Ay ay ay.

Suddenly, bars come down in front of the open end of the crate, imprisoning the girls.

LADY DUKE:
(*Sipping a mellow oolong from a rare expensive cup and counting out stacks of €'s*)
In short, the girls end up in debtor's prison. If only there was something I could do to help ...

MAERY:

(*Cont'd*)

It was in prison that I stopped apologizing for my existence. I added an "E" to the interior of my name, along with the Drachenfels insignia tattooed across my lower back. There's something very scary inside me that wants to come out – and I've decided I'm going to let it.

And anyway why shouldn't I write of monstehs. If this isn't the Underworld we're in, then I don't know what is ...

🎵 *SONG: DRUMS OF BATTLE, OF IMPRISONED WOMEN* 🎵
WHO WANT TO FIGHT

CHORUS OF IMPRISONED WOMEN:

(*Singing*)
Now I hear the drums of battle.
There is no one here to fight.

IMPRISONED WOMAN:

(*Shouting*)
Dark beast, we know you are there.
Why will you not make yourself known
so that we may fight you?

CHORUS OF IMPRISONED WOMEN:
Now I hear the drums of battle.
There is no one here to fight.

IMPRISONED WOMAN:

(*Shouting*)
Prison guard? Afraid of lady prisoners.
Lady prisoners who want to fight.

CHORUS OF IMPRISONED WOMEN:
Now I hear the drums of battle.
There is no one here to fight.

ALL:
We are wily.

CLARIE:
(*Shouting*)
We strip to nakedness and coat our skins
with baby oil so you'll never get a grip
and we fight that way.

CHORUS OF IMPRISONED WOMEN:
Now I hear the drums of battle.
There is no one here to fight.

MAERY:
(*Shouting*)
Clarie is dead weight, her specialty. Fight each other. Fight my
sisters instead of the beast itself – not appearing - will not
appear out of fear!

ALL:
(*Singing, screaming, fighting*)
Lady prisoners. We fight to the beat of the drums. (x2)
Lady prisoners.
We fight to the beat of the war drums.

Maery somehow escapes from prison, out from between the bars.
Her sisters help her, as her escape is their own only hope of release.

The Witnesses say the following lines to distract the
prison guards.

WITNESS 2: I've never talked to anyone about this. I think if I tell someone, they'll think I've completely lost it. I can't believe it myself.

WITNESS 1: I saw a shadow move

WITNESS 2: In his report he said that he felt as though he was "looking at a shadow." I was particularly interested to find out what he meant by that. The fact that its color was so uniform from head to toe, at least from a distance, reminded him of the uniformity of color in a man's shadow.

WITNESS 1: Once I couldnt see it anymore I decended the tower and walked through the bog in the same direction as the creature.

MAERY:
(*Later, out of prison but giving birth alone in exile*)
I don't know how I escaped. But it was just in time. For something new, old, and terrible was being born.
It got real quiet, too quiet. Those ghost babies headed for the old dark hills and were on the fade, and I entered a new exile and waited, and listened to the forest, while this thing that was trying to be born was worrying its way out.
(*Delirious, unseeing*)
I don't know where I was then, "these vague regions, utterly unlike the shores of the brilliant Rhine where scarcely a peak was left without a castle ... The dark ages, when they reached here, would have found no lights to extinguish, for none had ever burned here."[23]
And me? I can't stop writing ... even if I wished I could ...
... something's ... it's pushing, it wants ...

23. Quoted from *A Time Of Gifts: On Foot To Constantinople* by Patrick Leigh Fermor.

(She is panting.
Then, from another voice, which isn't hers)
I AM SHE WHO HASTENS THE BIRTH.

(Then again, as Maery)
Huh? What?

(But then, urgently, before she has time to think)

My Box of Keepsakes breaks open and spills all over the
ground – quite like the jar of pickles on the kitchen floor when
there was a kitchen - all the letters, the pedigrees, the charred
remains of Percy's heart, the locks of hair I saved representing
the shattered remnants of my own attempts at loving other
humans, the journal entries of all the terrible and dark
experiences I underwent while growing through terrible and
deadly femaledom, and LB's letters, and some strange Witness
testimonies that have been inserted into the slot for unknown
reasons, SPILT! into the dirt, all over the rocks. And I take it
all in hand, all these items which signify my only known life
and which now seem too strange to me, and regroup them,

(She does so, frantically ...)

re-form them into, into a figure I cannot identify – too huge to
be human! – and yet every bit as hideous as I sometimes feel
on the inside! – but which I recognize because it is one I HAVE
SEEN and HEARD and KNOWN BEFORE and causes the
hair to stand up on my arms and the back of my neck ... !
Whatever this is, it is made entirely of questions. I make
this and it defies understanding. The answer will only be
the inexplicable over and over and over again. And it is an
OFFERING. And ...
It will be a fight to keep my soul intact.

The Monster, now becoming fully manifest, lies on the ground.

Underneath her next speech, its enormous figure sits up, all of the items from the Box clinging to it, forming it, making it what it is. It joins in gradually with what Maery is saying. They speak the bold-faced text simultaneously.

MAERY:
*(Cont'd, with **Monster** joining in)*
There were some **certain textual volumes** I came across, and I read them from **the part** of the schloss **that isn't used**, where I could have **light**, and where they would not be **damaged by the elements.**

The Monster that Maery has composed of the contents of the Box of Keepsakes (letters, ink, locks of hair, charred remains of bodily organs of loved ones) slowly stands. The shape of his body: arms too long, sagittal crest, heavy brow. Huge. Mighty. And wild, unstoppable.

MONSTER:
(Taking the reins completely, now, from Maery)
The light coming through was from the gaps in the plywood that boarded up the windows. I could only read in the day, until I got some candles. I enjoyed lighting them at that hour when everyone else switches on the electric lights. It really got all the stories into my bowels. I would have died for these stories. I was outside of society, so it helped.

WITNESS 1: She notices something was hiding behind a tree.

WITNESS 2: we saw this gigantic figure.

WITNESS 1: As we got closer, I still could see it, because the moonlight was so bright.

WITNESS 2: It looked around the tree right at her and then poked back into hiding

WITNESS 1: It was at that point that I realized what the earlier sound was and a chill came over me.

The Monster yawns. He has just been born but is getting really sleepy.

MONSTER:
Ha! Just thinking of the darkness where I lived, without the license of permission. To be honest. I'm reluctant to talk about my private relationship to the nature of life, my life's relationship to science and ugh. That's where it gets really complex. It's different for me depending on which continent. In the Germanic, those dark Romantic days, I was a really irresponsible creation of humankind, a loner, created not on a castle operating table like in the movies but in a horse uterus with fermented (or rancid, depending on who you talk to) semen and body parts of various deceased bastards and criminals, in a crazy, crazy scientific process that no one should really be doing.
Joining together what was separate. My parts are twitching like a dog having a dream.

Lightning! Bundles of electric cables are glowing!

MONSTER:
(Cont'd)
Something's giving this sewed-together European-body-parts-body the idea that it should pull air into itself using the lung bags, and then push it out again, and that it's a good idea to repeat that, and there are angels and demons hanging around on each side, wondering what the hell is going on, thinking to lend a hand in squeezing and pulling on the heart chambers to suck up or expel blood – crusty, powdered, slightly moistened the soggy, sludge, then liquid thick or thin. And the brain? It's anybody's guess ... who shouldn't be a life but it is.

MAERY:

It was a bad dream I had when I was little, over and over again lying down asleep in the backseat of the car, I sat up and looked in the front seat there was no one there! The car was driving but no one driving it!! No mommy! No daddy! And it was always bright daylight.

MONSTER:

Ever catch yourself watching a vulture in the sky and then come totally awake when you realize it's an eagle you're watching? Or that's watching you? While you slaughter a yearling bull in its honor, its true identity unbeknownst? And then keeps circling you while you bathe in the half-frozen falls to wash the blood off? That's the kind of thing that makes you realize there's no right from wrong.

MAERY:

This pickup truck doesn't have a backseat, and anyway it's me who's driving. But here has been a fear of mine: that I'll be driving down a dark road at night and look in the rearview mirror and I'll see a – in the bed of my pickup truck – a – ah –

Maery's face drains with fear.

We hear, once again, the engine of the pickup truck we heard earlier. Far away, in an echo, with a strain of some music with lyrics on the subject of virginity on the radio.

The truck shifts from third gear to fourth.

MAERY:
When I entered the outer world
I stepped down very far
on the staircase.

MONSTER:
I share the vision of both eagle and vulture. I spot you from
high above – and I choose you.

MAERY:
I stepped much farther
than just downstairs – I kept stepping.

MONSTER:
You know it because you can feel it.

MAERY:
Past the basement.

MONSTER:
You can also communicate beyond the measurements.

MAERY:
Very, very far down. I began to go under, under ...

MONSTER:
You pick up on the same vibrations and disturbances as those
who live inside the Earth.

MAERY:
And I hear. I hear, with my second attention ...

We hear a lo-hi-pitched moan – inhuman.

MAERY:
(Cont'd, shouting into the darkness)
WHAT ARE YOU!? Did I MAKE you or did I just
CARRY you??

MONSTER:
Just like you could always feel who ruled the dark Germanic
hills before the Germans. Who waited on the farthest away

hillock in Wales. Who tilled the wildest secret land and hid the key to the women's prison from the King and then released them all after he fell asleep.

And what else. What other buried triumphs were carried in your own bone marrow and would rise up from underneath the ground, from out of the depths, from the horrors wrought by disconnected conquerors, to meet you. Heaven is a sterile krankenhaus. I'd rather laugh with the sinners than cry with the saints ...

MAERY:

I later come to realize that it was YOU! – the big creature walking around outside my lonely childhood bedroom window and who was also living inside ... of ... me. And that I'd truly never escape.

I can't stop writing and I can't stop driving ... even if I wished I could ...

I'm panting ... like a dog from the underworld ...

The Monster falls into a deep sleep, and his dream begins, in song.

MONSTER:
If dream is a reminiscence,
It's the reminiscence
Of a state preceeeeding life,
If dream is a reminiscence
Of a state of dead life,
A kind of mounting mourning before happiness happens

The love I knew did not live
But was on the way to re-living
The love I knew did not live
Prior existence aborted?
Or anterior death reembodied and then just abandoned?
Tell meeeeeeeeeee

CHORUS:
Cuz I'm lost in darkness, I'm lost in distaaaaannnnnce ...
God b'w'ye and T'Hell w'ye
(Goodbye and Hellow)
Take it eaaasy
Take it eeeeeeaasy
You gotta know that your sweet love drives me craazyyyyyy
Drives me crazy,
God b'w'ye and T'Hell w'ye
(Goodbye and Hellow)

I almost learned, clandestinely, to be human
I read the patriarchies, the victories, and the empires
(Sifted around in the ruins)
(Took it all literallyyy)
From belooooooooowwww

MONSTER & MAERY:
This nobility
This sorrowing spirit
This primordial nature
No father's merit
No mother's smiles
No memoryyyyyyyyyyyyyyyy
No memoryyyyyyyyyyyyyyyy

CHORUS:
I am lost in darkness and I'm lost in distaaaaannnnnce ...
God b'w'ye and T'Hell w'ye
(Goodbye and Hellow)
Take it eaaasy
Take it eeeeeeaasy
You gotta know that your sweet love drives me craazyyyyyy
drives me craazyyyyyy
God b'w'ye and T'Hell w'ye
(Goodbye and Hellow)

You drive me craazyyyyyy ...

◀ PART 2 ▶

INEVITABLE RECIPROCATION

> *Only see:*
> *Just at the light's edge, just before sunrise,*
> *Earth rumbled underfoot, forested ridges*
> *Broke into movement, and far howls of dogs*
> *Were heard across the twilight as the goddess*
> *Nearer and nearer came.*
>   *Hecate.*

- The Aeneid

11. ROAD TRIP: TO THE BURN ZONE

Maery is driving a pick-up truck and at the same time trying to write a journal entry onto a roll of stolen toilet paper on the dashboard.

Journal of Maery S. Square 63. Date Unknown.
Unseasonably warm.

I don't know what happened to my actual journal. I am now somehow in Modern-day dystopian America. There is an unfilled space, or interval. A missing chapter where I crossed the Atlantic. A cavity in the bone, a dislocation from who I am and what I've known, even from my own will. I have not chosen to be here. I was brought, without having given my consent. And I get the feeling I'm not the only one, and not the first to occupy this space between known and unknown, a state of oblivion and nothingness. And what now, that I have chosen to live and to fatalistically submit to uncertainty. I write this on a roll of stolen toilet paper on the dashboard of a pickup truck I am driving with my other

hand. I don't think the pickup truck is stolen,
I think it's from a bad dream I used to have in
childhood. But I'm not sure. I'm juggling a lot right
now, okay? Everything's mixed up. Nothing's what I
thought it was.

She grips the wheel with both hands for a moment, swerving to avoid something on the road ahead of her. She watches it pass and then it is behind her.

Journal of Maery S. Square 64. Unknown year.
Rogue storms, out-of-season.

I've seen something on the road ahead of me. I swerve
to miss it, and try to watch it as I pass.

WITNESS 1: The eyes were shining yellow in her headlights.

WITNESS 2: The witness stated that it was very tall over 6ft tall and had red eyes and a man like face.

The Lady Duke, from a golf cart, with opera glasses, looks on.

LADY DUKE:
It seems that the formal aesthetics of Gothic style have found their expression once again in a new point in history – this geography – forward in time and across the Atlantic Ocean, the GOTH SUBCULTURE, which **began in England during the early 1980s, and has continued to diversify and spread throughout the world. Its imagery and cultural proclivities indicate influences from 19th-century Gothic literature and**

Gothic horror films and has associated tastes in music, aesthetics, and fashion.

If we look at Maery now we can see the Wheel of the Gothic has come back around to the dystopic America of the Reagan-Bush-Thatcher era – responding at least in part to the plague of death and denial that was the AIDS crisis, just as one example. This gorgeous young sourpuss behind the wheel is redefining herself once again, at greater and higher risk each time.

Journal of Maery S. Square 65. Hurdling into modernity. Extreme changes in atmosphere.

And it is chasing me! At high speeds! It is a long-nurtured nightmare come true!!

THE VOICE OF THE MONSTER:
I'm behind you on the road and I'm right on your tail. You're doing the speed limit and that's not fast enough for me. FASTER BITCH FASTER!!

MAERY:
Look, it's just after dark. There's a reason the speed limit's 30 through here and I don't like to be intimidated just because that's how fast I'm going.

THE VOICE OF THE MONSTER:
I see you flip the rearview mirror up so my angry flashing highbeams don't blind you. That makes me worse. I climb out of my car and climb up into the back of your pickup truck. We are about to enter the Burn Zone. You think you hear something and look in your side view mirror to see my car careen off the shoulder and down into the deep drop of woods.

MAERY:
It was a shitty car.

MONSTER:
Your eyes are wide and moreverymore than concerned as you look at it crash into the trees and combust, then up in your rearview only to see my hoary face and rotten, toothy grin. Up close and personal. Hi. I see you see me. Remember me. And that makes the smile even uglier. F-uglier. I am in the back of your truck. We are in the Burn Zone.

Maery screams and it is possibly out of some incomprehensible triumph.

WITNESS 1: I would say when I first saw it, it was about 75 feet away

WITNESS 2: From across a meadow the crashing got louder and closer.

WITNESS 1: I realized that the bird was definitely placed there for me.

12. ROAD TRIP: FROM THE ASHES

The Monster sits in the back of the pickup and is transformed by a sudden desire for tenderness.

LADY DUKE:
(Her golf cart pulls up in front of an old church on the corner of 6th Avenue & 20th Street in Manhattan, NYC)
While it might have all begun in the UK, the Goth subculture was given a very special flavor in the US ... by the cultural and moralistic platitudes & residues of Puritanism and its very, very close co-influential proximity to the Satanic Panic of the 1970s. Take these sort of kids you'd see at the Limelight Club in the Peter Gatien days for an example – the most significant and infamous of all the Limelight locations – before it was a shopping mall or a gym ... Gothic revival architecture, by the way, that Episcopal Church of the Holy Communion across 6th Ave here at 20th Street, deconsecrated in the early 1970's. (I'll say. Doesn't it all come full circle if we pay attention –) Meanwhile, it's been a long, long night of aggression and defensive driving for Maery and her Monstrous Creation –

MONSTER:
And now I find Uh-oh. I'm suddenly findingfind now that I've changed my mind (I have a mind) I desperately want tenderness from you. From YOU – My road rage enemy!!

WITNESS 1: At that instant her uncle quietly exclaimed "msnapeo"[24] and her aunt told all the children to lie down in the back of the wagon while she (the aunt) threw a blanket over them.

MONSTER:
Now I just want to go with you. I justcan stilljust want tenderness. Exposure to tenderness.

WITNESS 1: She said that her uncle just turned the wagon around on the road and headed them back to home.

MONSTER:
(I know this might seem like something of an abrupt 180° swerve from the ferocious aggression of just a couple seconds ago.)
I don't know if it's too late. Except that it's never too late. YOU HEAR ME? I said it's never too late to back off from murderous, self-righteous aggression. I'm just not gonna be worried about consistency here.

WITNESS 2: As an innocent child I was not afraid.

The truck drives on, Maery at the wheel.

The Monster turns around from his earlier threatening stance and rides with his feet dangling off the back of the truckbed. He looks at his own body, comparing what he sees in this, Part II, with the way he was made in Part I.

Their progress across states of being, states of mind, is traced along the interstate, on the MAPESTRY, which is echoed, by county, in a Bigfoot research Map at the Witness station, during the following.

24. A Stony/Assinboine word for a Sasquatch, translating literally to "big people," from this following report: https://www.bfro.net/GDB/show_report.asp?id=1422

MONSTER:
Across the Atlantic (on the new continent. New to who? New
to YOU), I've been there the whole time. A woodwose. That I
once lived among youse but have become instead a watcher.
A wild thing of the woods I'm totally natural, part of a tight
community, called an animal though the real people know I am
also a people.

I'm helpless here without you as I "chase" you through all the
states – states of mind, states of being, states of the United
States and Canada – you're the one carrying the torch out here
on the Interstate. I don't know how you can see in this total
darkness – especially with that Veil! – it's too dark even for me!
I can't see a goddamn thing. Except for you.

*Their progress across states of being, states of mind, is traced
along the interstate on the MAP though The Lady Duke is
strangely absent:*

*ME, NH, VT, NY, PA, OH, KY, IN, IL, IA, NE, MT, ID, WA, OR,
NV, UT, CO, NM, TX, OK, AK, LA, MS, AL, FL, GA, Fear, Rage,
Aggression, Self-Righteousness, Disgust, Exhaustion, Dogged
Determination, Frustration, Over-Functioning, Surrender,
Tenderness, Empathy, Hastening, Rebirth of Self ... Awe ...
Appearing, Seeming, Becoming, Turning, Beingness, Receptiveness,
Sensing, Feeling, Intuiting, Perceiving ...*

MAERY:
I hasten the screaming engine of this chunky American rig
at high speeds into some dystopian Underworld – driving us
over one crossroads after another. I encounter you each time –
the Other – as you watch me. I feel you watching me. At each
crossroads, watching becomes seeing. I feel you watching me,
and then I feel seen by you. Yet I know this Veil will never be
lifted by any mortal. So what does that make you, buddy?

They drive and drive until their rage is spent. At a truck stop at dawn, someplace in the deep South.

MONSTER:

It's a long ride. I wake up and you're still driving. It's morning before you ever stop. Stop draggin my. Stop draggin my. Stop draggin my. But you don't join in. We pull over for gas and (hopefully) breakfast. But now it seems like you've forgotten I'm here. You act as if you've forgotten I'm even here.

MAERY:

Hah! Believe me, I'd love to forget.
(Her boots hit the asphalt and she gets a jolt from the ground)
Whoa. Some kind of horror unfolded in this history.
Underneath these roads and parking lots. I feel it coming up through the asphalt and into my boots. And I get the feeling it's not even history. Ok.
(She shakes it off and recomposes)
I'm going to go in to this truck stop and take a hot shower. Maybe buy some air fresheners to hang from my rearview mirror, or some remote control toys. I don't know. I'll decide once I'm in there. Some kind of clothing with thethatthe new photographic-looking camouflage. See what they have on display in the aisles. See what I think.

MONSTER:

Alright. I'm going to go foraging over in the pet relief area. I might eat dog shit and I might not. By the time you come back out I'll be back here waiting for you at the truck. It's fine that you're not inviting me to come in to the truck stop with you.

MAERY:

(From inside the truck stop)
So this is the "New World" – ha! More like New Underworld. Big trucks. Fast food. Risky maneuvers. Lot of power for a

people so careless and capricious – same as putting a toddler behind the wheel of an aeroplane. What the hell is that anyway, an aeroplane.
(*She looks around. People are watching her*)
It seems to me that the whole construct, under its own Veil of obliviousness, teeters on the edge of absolute, downright Oblivion.
What the hell is everybody looking at?
What are you all looking at me like that for? Am I scared of you? Or am I scaring you? Whose Veil!? Whose Veil!? What are these, cigars? There's an Underworld underneath this Underworld that you've all created your damned selves. It's much less civilized than we were even two hundred years ago. And two thousand years ago for that matter. It's like a goddamn free-for-all. We won't be here long, or at least I won't.

MONSTER:
(*Trying to adjust, but*)
I still feel lost. I know if somebody gets scared of me over at the pet relief area and complains, that she isn't going to help me. It would be against something she's not ready to go against.

MAERY:
(*At the cash register, plunking a silk bundle of gold coins onto the counter and telling the check-out man as if she's talking about the weather or a sports match*)
These people are so haunted by their own landscape.
The amount of unknown info and unknown stories is overwhelming. It scares the crap out of them and they can't – or won't – identify it. So they lash out at it with plows and chains and guns and drills and loud tailpipes and tasers and tear gas and marketing and yoga and tractors and garbage and investments and cuss words and policies and bulldozers.

MONSTER:

I go anyway and do my foraging and the sun isn't up yet
so people aren't sure what they're seeing. I do my
thing undisturbed.
I do think she'll let me back in the truck as long as I am
waiting there when she comes out.

MAERY:

I guess I'll get some tobacco for my pipe ... wait. Where's my
pipe? Where's my Box!?
Ok, I should probably call and check in with my sisters ... (*going
to a pay phone*) who are still in prison but they are super pissed
and haven't seen it ...
(*Speaking into the phone's receiver*)
Hello, Clarie? Fanny? HOWZIT!!
And suddenly a big piece of plexiglass drops down in front of
me. (*Covering the phone with one hand, whispering*)
What is 'plexiglass'?
Fanny and Clarie are like, screeching -
"How do you THINK it is? We're still in JAIL!"
Oh boy. They're really yelling in my ear.
They want to know where the hell I went.
(*Covering the receiver again*) What can I even tell them?
(*Into the phone*) Uhh ... I just had to go. There was something I
needed to ... birth ....
(*Aside*) Now they want the Box Desk ...
(*Listening to the phone*)
They think some of the papers in there might help them prove
their identity and credibility, and get them out of jail ...
(*Into the phone*)
Well, I was actually calling to ask you the same thing! It's not
there in the jail with you guys? It's not with LB? Well, then is
it at one of the campingplätze? I just bought a nice cigar box to
use in the meantime ... It's all they had ...
Which brand?

Oh. Which platz?
Oh. Uh, I guess that mouldy one?
Yeah, true, I guess they were all pretty mouldy lol.
(*More screaming from the other end of the line*)

Rechte oder linke seite ....
Eh, linke.
(*Trying to remember*)

Rheincamping Siebengebirgsblick? (*Aside, covering the receiver, interpreting*)
Seven Mountains Vista.

Lido-Camping Bad Hönningen? (*Aside, covering the receiver, interpreting*)
Campingplatz Moselbogen?
(auf der Mosel)?
Bend at the River Mosel.
Camping Wolfsmühle?
(auf dem Lahn)? (*Aside, covering the receiver, interpreting*)

Campingplatz Ziehfurt? Mill for Wolves.
(*Aside, covering the receiver, interpreting*)

Campingplatz Uferwiese? Beat it About.
(*Aside, covering the receiver, interpreting*)

Campingpark Sonneneck? On the Other Hand.
Campingplatz auf der Loreley? (*Aside, covering the receiver, interpreting*)
Redneck Campingpark.

I don't know. I can't remember ...
(*Aside*)
I need to give up on this phone call.
(*She hangs up and lights one of the cigars, dumping the rest into one of the single-use plastic shopping bags that grows on trees here in the New UnderWorld, this one emblazoned with the CROSSROADS TRUCKSTOP logo*)

I'll check in with them later. For right now, literally all I have is exploration. So I just need to move on.

She puts the remainder of her belongings into the cigar box.

Meanwhile, the following Witness Testimonies are the first new thing she adds to this downgraded Box. She does so resignedly ...

WITNESS 1: He could tell something scared the hell out of me. He told me to keep driving until I got home.

WITNESS 2: I started for home and I made it back to Thompson in 50 minutes. I was doing 65-70 MPH. This truck is not suppose to go over 55 MPH but at that point in time I didn't care I just wanted to be home. As soon as I got home I opened the fridge and grabbed a beer. The noise I was making woke my roommate and he asked said how come you are so white and why are you drinking so early in the morning. I told him what happened and he believed me to my surprise.

I stayed off Prov Road 280 for a week.

MONSTER:
(*Sing-talking along to the music on the radio*)
There's peoples runnin' round loose in the world.

Ain't got nothin' better to do.

Than make a meal of some bright-eyed kid.

You need someone lookin' after you.

I know you really want to tell me goodbye.

To this day June 18, 2000. I will always look around for the time I am out of my truck till I am back home.

MONSTER:
I know you really want to be
your own girl.

TOM PETTY & STEVIE NICKS, or some perhaps rough approximation, come crashing in to close out the scene: "BABY YOU COULD NEVER LOOK ME IN THE EYE / NOW YOU BUCKLE WITH THE WEIGHT OF THE WORDS / STOP DRAGGIN' MY / STOP DRAGGIN' MY / STOP DRAGGIN' MY HEART AROUND"

T

13. ROAD TRIP: FALLING IN LOVE WITH THE HUMAN

Those who spot the Monster in the treeline think he is Bigfoot. And so ... he is.
Their journey is traced on the MAP. They are covering much territory, heading Northward, toward Canada.

WITNESS 1: It had to have known what we were going to do next.

WITNESS 2: We could see

WITNESS 1: and while it ran I could see

WITNESS 2: in the trees.

WITNESS 1: wider and taller than a person.

WITNESS 2: left arm was massive, bigger than

WITNESS 1: In less than 5-6 seconds

MONSTER:
I'm just sort of starting to hope that she comes out soon.

Not that I care. Who sees me.

But I – maybe she does.

And I seem to suddenly care if she cares.

If she cares, I care. I care if she cares.

WHETHER she cares.

WITNESS 2: it looked at me while darting across the road

WITNESS 1: at least 8-8.5 feet tall,

WITNESS 2: an adult cow but in a human form.

WITNESS 1: you could hear the crashing of it moving

WITNESS 2: Saw leaves and stuff that came down

WITNESS 1: instantly got chills

WITNESS 2: thought only my wife and I saw it.

WITNESS 1: I stood there

WITNESS 2: I stood there

WITNESS 1: I stood there

WITNESS 2: Daddy what was that.

WITNESS 1: The road being dirt, and because of the rain,

WITNESS 2: With how steep the area

WITNESS 1: I think it was very intelligent.

MONSTER:
I'm finding suddenly that.
I care.

Regardless of whether she cares or not.

Or would, if she knew that I am capable of caring.

If she cares.

I care if she cares, for myself I don't care if people see me.

But if she cares if people see me, then I care too.

I don't think I've ever experienced this kind of subtlety before.

I find myself watching her for clues as to what she cares about.

I stand next to her at the edge of the woods and I look off toward where she's looking.

WITNESS 2: through the brush-brush, and trees.

MONSTER:
That groundhog?
That female duck?

WITNESS 1: I told her I was going to pull the truck onto the edge of the road.

What about that little boy getting hurt?

WITNESS 2: it had . so there was a ridge of dirt on both sides

And then I find my own way to care about those things too.

WITNESS 1: and the look it gave me had power in it

WITNESS 2: we sat quietly in the truck

And I do my own version of caring about what's happening, or is going to happen.

WITNESS 1: we sat quietly in the truck

WITNESS 2: we sat quietly in the truck

🎵 *SONG: CANADIAN FOREST LOCATIONS,* 🎵
TO EXPERIENCE THE WILDERNESS OF LOVE BY

They keep driving and everything becomes suddenly saturated and vivid.

Early morning, cool,
Pine and cedar. Lakeside
Fallen rotting stumps and trees,
We came to a meadow

Midnight dark and clear.
Fir and hemlock and maple
You can almost look across the valley
Across the mouth of the river

CHORUS:
Pine, spruce, alder, and hemlock trees.
Lake dead calm air was steep.
Pine, spruce, alder, and hemlock trees.
Perfection of the water.

Late afternoon sun behind
Water falls near end of lake
All the time looking
Forest sign of movement

CHORUS:
Pine, spruce, alder, and hemlock trees.
Lake dead calm air was steep.
(All the) pine, spruce, alder, and hemlock trees.
Reflection off the water.
Reflection off the water.
Reflection off the water.

Pine, spruce, alder, and hemlock trees.

J

MONSTER:
Now we all know that somewhere along the line, darlin.
The vulture of impending death becomes the eagle of
transformation. And Germanic. Becomes ...
German Romanticism ...
Love isn't the kind of destroying I was looking for, but it just
might do...

*For some reason the map is showing that they are back in the
Mittelrhein section of Germany, in a small village at the foot
of the Seven Mountains range. Must be a glitch or something.
Nevertheless, it's utterly charming. Delightful.*

MAERY:
How did we get back here again? It's still summer. I want to go
to the festival in this town. It's a full moon. They've picked out
the wine maiden. I know it isn't me – that's ok. I just like to be
here and learn the songs.

MONSTER:
Ok I'll take you. I haven't been back there for a while, but we
can put the time dimensions together and the difference in
relationships to life aside just for one night.

MAERY:
What could it harm?

They laugh a little together.

MONSTER:
(*Glancing around*)
Nobody seems to notice, or if they notice, they don't seem to mind. Together once again, back on German soil. And I so much enjoy the music.

MAERY:
I sit on your lap .... And later ... let's take a walk through the village.

MONSTER:
I can't believe my luck. The houses are really so charming.

MAERY:
Look at that man inside on his computer! What is he doing that he is not at the festival??

They laugh together.

MONSTER:
This little lane between two of the houses, it goes right through – past their garden walls covered in vines –

MAERY:
Oh – the lane becomes a path climbing up into the woods. A forest tunnel through the dark boughs overhanging. We climb and climb in the darkness of an overcast night, compelled forward, each on our two hind legs, by the suggestion of a clearing up ahead, farther uphill.

MONSTER:
By now perhaps people are returning to their homes in the

village below. For us, discoveries follow one upon another in such a way that they seem to resemble thoughts, and so begin to feel pre-determined.

MAERY:
In the clearing, a hut. A hutte. It is dark inside.

MONSTER:
This is the night you really scare the shit out of me.
You're really scaring the shit out of me.

MAERY:
I think I'm was just going to put on a little show, for a laugh, but it becomes much more serious. This is serious. I am pulled into something else. Some other knowledge.

MONSTER:
I look out into the darkness and see your strange gleaming body and your undone hair swaying through the brambles, bent over, hands almost reaching the ground. I don't know what to do. So I take my own shirt off and just have a seat inside the hutte. I have this feeling like you are lost forever.

MAERY:
(*Remembering there is freedom and power here*)
I'm looking out into a black expanse and know I belong there and am never coming back. I need no clothes or food from society ever again. Why should I ever try to sleep in some apartment or motel room somewhere ever again? Hold a job? I've never needed any of that stuff. It just gets in the way.

MONSTER:
(*Singing*)
Well, you really got me this time.

MAERY:
Part of me will always live in the forest and survive off of foods I can not normally eat, like roots! I am incredibly strong. I move about only at night, and during the day I sleep unseen. I guess – something tells me instinctively that I should avoid humans. At all costs.

MONSTER:
(*Speaking*)
And it's like here is where we can be both. Because what I was made of that was dead comes back to life and memory. And I'm still united with what is outside human understanding. The way you are right now, as I chase you through the night at unnatural lightning speeds but never catch you is that I'm still ... natural.

MAERY:
And so what am I?

MONSTER:
You are beyond the natural. Beyond, but running parallel.

MAERY:
So I am meta-natural? Para-natural?

MONSTER:
Para-meta. And so super. I see you ranging out – outside of the Veil, yet still engaged, with or without your clothes on.

MAERY:
I don't know what convinces me to put my clothes back on and go back.

MONSTER:
I know the feeling. The next day you were covered in welts and scratches from the sharp vegetation. Still engaged. Entangled.

You told me at the café that you thought you may have inadvertently traveled, not only to Germany the night before, but to the moon's womb and become a witch.

Percy S., her since-deceased husband, appears. He is very soggy and with strange tentacles hanging out of his waistcoat, and also possibly out of his face.

PERCY:
(*Floating in on a convection current*)
I never knew about this story, darling.

Lights out.

LADY DUKE:
(*Climbing through the brambles with a flashlight OR back in the Lecture Hall*)
Oh my goodness – just as we were putting the "Romantic" back into the "Dark Romanticism" end of the Gothic, somehow Maery's deceased husband Percy has appeared! He is quite soggy and with strange tentacles hanging out of his waistcoat, and, it looks like, possibly also out of his face... it will be exciting to see what happens!

They turn uneasily to look to the right. Lights out.

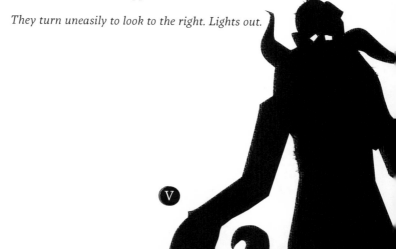

V

Percy again appears standing, in the same stance and position as before, to their right. A moment of assessment.

The Monster abruptly exits, crashing through the branches and screaming horribly.

Percy tries several tactics beyond just the brandishing of his arresting counter-tenor, including the suggestion that he could be a famous Bigfoot researcher in a new life, and prove/own/ dominate her Monster's existence.

MAERY:
Percy. What are you doing here. You don't have the constitution for the U.S. of A.

PERCY:
I miss you, Maery. Is there anything wrong or surprising in that? I've searched for you on the docks and beaches of every major and minor waterway in Europe.

MAERY:
You crossed the Atlantic?

PERCY:
I'm a lost sea creature. I guess that's what happens when your funeral was a pagan beach bonfire. Every time I become afraid

I squirt out some kind of foul inky liquid. And there is so much to fear down in the darkest deep ... I'm doing a terrible lot of squirting, it's dreadful ... I feel depleted, Maery ...

MAERY:
I can hardly see anything it's snowing so much.

She holds out her hands and face to receive the falling snow.

PERCY:
Didn't you hear what I said? I was talking about my funeral.

MAERY:
I heard you.

PERCY:
Darling!

MAERY:
I remember. The beach bonfire funeral pyre. It was LB's idea.

PERCY:
Don't you remember my heart was still there and didn't burn, Maery? // And you plucked it from the charred carcass and did something with it. Held it up to the skies, or ate it. // You, Maery, who I plucked from the tree of innocence, virtue, and virginity. // Brilliant girl. I took you from the arms of your Father and adored you very, very much. Now you are so expanded and I have remained the same, nearly as virginal in death as you were in that past life.

MAERY:
(*Reluctantly*)
// Yes ...

MAERY:
// Oh, come on!

MAERY:
// Ugh.

෴ SONG: *THE THIRD CHORUS OF GHOSTED CHILDREN* ෴

PERCY:
And I am here with all the
All the dead children, ours and Clarie's.
Ours and Clarie's.
Swimming all around in
Around both water and air.
They want you and Clarie to know
That they forgive you,
And that they are with you,
All of the time,
All of the time.

• ෴

MAERY:
And Fanny?

PERCY:
Yes, we see her sometimes. But she's with another group.

MAERY:
And who else?

PERCY:
And there were voices – I told you! – voices in the deep!

MAERY:
Yes. I think I know. Lost astronomers and physicians and
philosophers and priests, authors, engineers, statesmen and
stateswomen and matriarchs and tactician warrior queens.

Those who could not bear the unknown of the non-place,
of the lacuna, or maybe who knew all too well what it all might
be adding up to …

LADY DUKE:
(*Butting in*)
And I'd like to take a moment to appreciate this crossing
Maery has made into the world of another, contemporary
Gothic – or 'Goth' – style. It's been right here all along, but
I can't seem to locate it in any of my accepted, authoritative
sources. And as for myself, I can't quite put a finger on it …

Maery steps in and brushes The Lady Duke aside.

MAERY:
Allow me.

Maery gives the definition for Afro Goth movement and style[25]
herself, in her own words.[26]

MAERY:
(*Cont'd*)
As I traverse this country, I smell something rotten – some

---

25. https://medium.com/@janelane_62637/african-and-caribbean-culture-is-the-
foundation-of-the-gothic-movement-c3ba89bff31c

   https://www.vice.com/en_us/article/939mb3/theres-nothing-more-goth-than-
being-black

   https://pioneerworks.org/programs/afro-gothic/

   http://www.darkview.be/nieuws/2377-black-smoke-the-afro-goth-sub-culture

26. Mary Shelley never wrote a definition for the Afro Goth movement that we
know of, and this definition owes much to scholar Kobena Mercer as quoted on
the Pioneer Works gallery website, for their 2018 exhibit of *PÒTOPRENS: The
Urban Artists of Port-au-Prince.* The Afro-Gothic here refers to "an aesthetic
means of coping with the trauma of colonial slave history … Combining
the African diaspora imaginary with the European literary genre, the term
describes both beauty and terror, sex and violence, a 'slave sublime' haunted by
figures like the ghost or zombie … which function as allegor[ies] of black life
under colonialism."

decayed Baroque, some hoax besmirching the ideals of
Neoclassical pillars at the courthouse, the school, the governor's
mansion. Here, and deep down in that ocean I was brought
across without agreeing to come – and within my own self!
– there is a collective haunting, going back twenty and more
generations. It goes unacknowledged and unrepaired, largely
ignored by those who hold the chequebooks and the policies,
who do not see what the problem is. It is an inestimable loss
of all that was taken without consent, and it has not yet even
been properly grieved.

Therefore I now adorn myself in mourning for unknown and
unspoken losses of life, history, heritage, language, identity,
free will, children, energy, avocation, and relationship to
ancestors, land, country. This open and ornate display of grief
makes visible these losses. I open the intricate fan of my black
feathers. You see my tiger's stripes expand and cover the whole
cat. I demand acknowledgement and repair on which healing
depends. I pounce. I make reclamation of original power.

LADY DUKE:
Mmm.

MAERY:
It's something you and those like you have always never
known, and yet been a part of all the same. It haunts you, even
now. It rises up out of the ground!

LADY DUKE:
Oh! Whhhhhhat!?

MAERY:
That's right. You heard me. And by the way. My soul is still
intact, and never gets corrupted. My identity is a different
matter, however. That's what's veered off the rails, splintered,
and careened into parts unknown. Let's not confuse the two.

He's right. I am ALL selves. Para. Meta. Super.
Let's not mince words about what went down last night.
I re-became She Who Works Her Will.
She Who Brings the Coolness of Night to the Scorched Land.
She Who Hastens the Birth.
Triple Creatrix of the Celestial Planets and Cosmos.
She who encounters you.
She who is all that has been and all that will be.
No mortal has ever lifted my Veil.
Wisdom of dark places and Warrior Goddess of crossroads,
levels of knowledge.
Titan. Olympian. Male and female on either side of my body.
I am the first woman who populates the Earth and then moves
to the Moon to rest. I am Silver Wheel of the Year and
Web of Fate.
I am myself and my sisters – all parts of the Ocean: Surface,
Depths, Moon. Mother to all the Fish. Turbulence. Inexplicable
Dreams. I am vegetation, I am Sweet Water.
Selene. Artemis. Persephone. Hecate. Mawu. Arawa.
Andriamahilala. Ngame. Khonsu. Yemanya. Oshun. Abnoba
River Goddess. Abena. For children born on Tuesday – I was
born in Accra, Ghana and I can tell you it is Tuesday.
All. All.

MONSTER:
I'm with you on all of this.

MAERY:
(*Turning to him, and all the Primordial Waters turning with her*)
Yes, you certainly are. If I am she who makes and remakes the
world. Then you must be my consort who stewards all things
living and growing –

MONSTER:
If only I could do my job –

KALEIDoSCOPE of images!!! Emotions crystalized into the shapes of snowflakes, forming highly intelligent structures, falling all around them in the form of television static.

PERCY:
(*From off-right*)
A-hem. M-Maery? I want you to know how very sorry I am to have not left you with a penny.

MAERY:
Well, whatever.
We're traveling on the interstate now, one state of being to another, state of mind to another, to another. What's the harm.

PERCY:
You know if I had made it through that storm that night, and if I were still alive today, I could work in the bio-tech industry in Central New Jersey. I'd live in a brown apartment complex and my bachelor's pad would have white walls and black leather-ish couches. The kind with slouchy-looking layered cushions. I wouldn't be as well read. I'd be an analytic-type person. But I'd also know how to give back. I am telling you that I would be a volunteer for the New Jersey Department of Fish, Game, and Wildlife and that I would do many expeditions for unknown things in the woods, mostly in the Pine Barrens.

MAERY:
(*Barely listening*)
But you don't get to become any of those things, Percy. Because you died.

PERCY:
If I could track this Monster of yours, Maery ... prove its existence? Conquer? Conquer it by empirical proof? Capture? Capture it? Find a way to subdue, explicate, define ... Surely,

there must be some perfectly reasonable scientific explanation for all this ...

MAERY:
You're a monster yourself, Percy. Look at you. A sea monster, // and a ghost. You're in no condition to be expanding any empires, reasonable or otherwise ...

PERCY:
// Cre-ature. A sea creature of some kind. And furthermore. Don't you hear those tender strains, Maery? They're playin' our song.

MAERY:
(*Incredulous*)
Do I remember this one?

PERCY:
Why of course you do! It's the one where the loving, doting husband edits his sweetest bride's little toilet paper manuscript, in his chesty, competitive countertenor ...

MAERY:
Hmm. Well it does sound like a love duet. About control.

PERCY:
It just has so much potential, Maery. Come. Let us hear it in your own dulcet tones ...

It's Maery S. singing (from the left-hand column) with Percy's chesty, competitive countertenor (singing from the right-hand column), who always edited/embellished her writings for her. It's the same chords as "Onward Up" with actor choices determining the phrasing.

Percy edits Maery's manuscript in ...

SONG: A LOVE DUET. ABOUT CONTROL.

MAERY:	PERCY:
Talked	conversed
Hot	inflamed
Smallness	minuteness
End	extinction
Inside	within
Tired	fatigued
Die	perish
Leave out	omit
Add to	augment
Poverty	penury
Mind	understanding
Ghost-story	tale of superstition
About on a par	of nearly equal interest and utility
We were all equal	neither of us possessed the slightest preeminence over the other
Wrapping the rest	depositing the remains

LADY DUKE:

Percy finds that Maery has become a lot for him to handle in this new phase of her life, and this match is a draw.

The Monster has run off for now, but eventually he will have to circle back and square off with Percy. Time is the only matter, and for Percy who is not only deceased, but afloat and adrift in the ocean, time is a non-issue.

WITNESS 1: But we can't deny what we saw. I have to believe it because it was real.

WITNESS 2: It left me with more questions than answers.

WITNESS 1: I'm a father of 2 and a first aid attendant for the IWA union and I'm not a drug user or drinker so I know what I saw.

WITNESS 2: Now I will tell you right now that I am an avid hunter and nobody can tell me because I have hunted and shot every season since 1986.

WITNESS 1: This was different. And very eerie. Made the hair stand up on my arms.

WITNESS 2: I worked at the largest taxidermy facility in Canada for years and continued with my own business after (a total of 30 years experience).

WITNESS 1: I can't describe how I felt after seeing the creature.

WITNESS 2: I will never forget that, nor would I ever return there again. It makes the hair on my neck stand on end to this day.

WITNESS 1: what we seen and smelled will be remembered for the rest of our lives.

The Monster stops off at the Witness station and intimidates the Witnesses by pounding on the roof of the station and screaming and crashing around outside. The Witnesses are terrified and evacuate through the door on the other side into a truck parked near Maery's.

Maery S. is meanwhile sitting on the back of the truck bed where the Monster had been sitting, once upon a time, when they first abducted one another, and is dressed again in her period garb, but that which is all made of photographic type camouflage material. She smokes the same dainty pipe as LB smoked at the top of the blick earlier on, and polishes her musket.

MAERY:
Why DID I come back, anyway?
This old truck where we first abducted one another.
(*Singing quietly and vaguely to the radio songs*)
… I've come to listen for the sound
of the trucks as they move down
out on old I-95.
And pretend that it's the ocean
coming down to wash me clean,
to wash me clean.
Baby do you know what I mean.

When in this life will I liberate myself as I was in those other lives? Take down the boundaries around my progress and my prowess as erected by Percy, by my father, by the strictures of empirical thought & method, of corporate or institutional empire building altogether? If you judge me by the contents of this cigar Box, there isn't that much of me left really. A few faded receipts, a Bic lighter, some postal stamps, expired driver's license and registration, permit to carry a concealed intertemporal musket, and a damp stack of Witness Testimonies held together with an old hair scrunchie. A bunch of sets of keys to places I never owned – I don't know what they unlock anymore. Not a whole lot to show for all the trouble, I guess.

She grabs another cigar from the glove compartment and lights it with the Bic.

LADY DUKE:
(*From her golf cart, which is passing by the interstate rest area*)
Oh! A landscape painter! *En plein air!*
Oh! And is that MAERY S.!? Well, maybe I'd better pull over ...
Oh, YOO-HOOOO! Maeryyyyy!

MAERY:
With the help of a big, empowering musical number here, I just know I could get free, I could run away from the scary mansion, in my nightgown, into the night, and find a way to work my will again.

No musical number begins here, however. Instead, The Lady Duke approaches, in traveling garb.

LADY DUKE:
(*To the general assembly*)
Oh, hello. Do you remember me from earlier? Lady Jane Williams. Doris Duke.
(*To Maery*)
I've always thought you were so funny. You know you could really be doing stand-up. And it would be so funny. You'd do it in the way only you can!
Eh, by the way. That's 50 cents for the tobacco in that cigar.

Maery S. grunts and hands it over. The Lady Duke walks over to an artist who is strangely painting something nearby with an easel and gives it to him. Or puts it in the pocket of his painter's smock.

LADY DUKE:
What are you painting anyway?

PAINTER:
Oh, just a forest scene ...

MAERY:
At a roadside rest stop??

PAINTER:
As good a place as any, I suppose ...

LADY DUKE:
Have you ever applied for any grants or fellowships?

PAINTER:
Well ... maybe I could.

MAERY:
Wait a minute – what's that!?

PAINTER:
What! Where!

MAERY:
(*Referring still to the painting*)
There! Right there at the tree line!

PAINTER:
Oh, I DON'T KNOW – I just paint what I see!

LADY DUKE:
What! What is it!

MAERY:
It's a figure! A dark, bulky figure. Too large to be that of a man!

LADY DUKE:
Where!? I don't see it.

MAERY:
(*To the painter*)
Keep painting!
(*Now pointing at the painting*)
There! Right there! Do you see it??

LADY DUKE:
I don't know. It looks like it could be someone in a suit.

PAINTER:
(*Offended*)
No it doesn't!

MAERY:
Keep GOING! Keep painting! Keep steady now – you're wobbling too much!!

PAINTER:
(*Defensive*)
I am not!

The Lady Duke jerks her head around suddenly, then whispers loudly:

LADY DUKE:
Did you hear that.

MAERY:
(*Also jerking her head around*)
I sure did. I definitely heard that. You're damn right I heard it.

(*To the painter*)
You. Keep painting. Something's starting to form. It's …

PAINTER:
Huge. A bear?

MAERY:
No. A bear doesn't walk like that.
On two legs like that? No.

PAINTER:
(*Painting furiously*)
Oh my gawd. Are you seeing what I'm seeing?

LADY DUKE:
It's coming close! We're too close!

They exit. The painter keeps trying to paint while running away.
Maery is frozen to the spot.

LADY DUKE:
Maery, are you coming?

MAERY:
Yeah, I guess.
Yeah. I guess I'll run away too …

She runs away too, leaving the cigar Box behind.

17. PERCY's REPRISALS,
AND A SONG TO BECOME HUMAN BY.

The MAP shows continued progress on the Interstate.

The Monster walks onto the stage, stands a bit dejectedly, looking all around him.

MONSTER:
See this is what happens. People are just about to get some good footage – some real, indisputable evidence – and they get too scared, and they run away. Or else the technology somehow weirdly breaks down. Technology will always fail you and really, in most cases. Even watercolors. Or acrylics. Even oils! And believe me, I know. I'm here a lot of the time. Your home is built on hallowed ground, hoss. And I'm only heard when I want to be heard. Everything is very subtle. You're watching so many movies and television shows these days that you're starting to need everything spelled out for you, that's your problem. You can't hold your attention on anything. You need to be told what to think and feel. Or where does it leave you?

The Monster sees Maery's cigar Box on the truck bed. Picks it up and examines it.

MONSTER:
I hope that's not too forward of me to observe out loud.

About you.

Another moment. He suddenly screams and bellows and crushes/ throws the cigar Box and its contents.

Maery comes running back on. She is saying:

MAERY:
~~~ I don't know why I ran away. The truth is I have to love. I open out of necessity.
(*Then, seeing what he has done*)
Oh no, what have you done!? There wasn't much left of that old Box but it contained my identity! It was my father's! And then it was my husband's! And then he died!

The Monster screams and howls again into the air.

MAERY:
Now you've completely smashed who I am! Who I was supposed to always be! Who I had always meant to be!

He howls again. He throws his way-huge arms up and falls to his knees. Maery rushes to him, instinctually, and takes his big stinking monster body in her arms.

MAERY:
There, there. Let me embrace you. You are my Creation, even if you are a hideous one and even if you destroy everything else in my life!

MONSTER:
It isn't easy. I know. I know everything you've been through. Why shouldn't you write of Monsters.

They cry together for a few moments.

MAERY:
You know, I'm just thinking. It's really important that I find my original Box of Keepsakes.

He takes her hand and puts it on his own heart area.

MONSTER:
I vow to help you.

By now the sun is setting in a blaze of glory, just behind them, into the tree tops at the edge of the picnic area.

The Monster moves off to the thick brush behind the landscaping of the picnic area, foraging for scraps and berries.

It is Maery who watches him this time, from atop a picnic table.

As he rummages and gathers and puts things in his mouth to eat, broken pieces from the shattered Box drop away out of his increasing tufts of fur, clattering onto the asphalt, and thudding onto the grass and dirt. In this way his natural hairy body emerges.

MAERY:
He *is* my box of keepsakes, or he has been up until this moment ...
I watch the parts of him that were built from my own identity and life experience drop away onto the pavement, as he becomes his own thing, as his natural hairy body emerges, as he becomes his own Force of Nature.
As I watch, as I see him, a rising feeling in my solar plexus tells me that I am witnessing a Force of Love in the Universe that ultimately has nothing to do with me, but that justifies my existence in the mark that it leaves for the future.
I begin to see how the Past and the Future converge into the Present Moment, in each new moment that he lives and acts

unexpectedly and unpredictably, and independently of me. That kind of Life can't be created working with formulas.

He takes my history with him out into the world, where it will become, and be shared by many others.

His scary actions make the marks of the life I have lived within myself.

As I see him move away from me, into the world on his own terms, the rising feeling in my solar plexus is capped by a heavy and bottomless sorrow in my heart's cavernous cavity. That reaches all the way to the rock bottom of my own personal Underworld, where I conceived him.

And yet he lives, and doesn't die ... hideous and terrifying as he may be to behold ...

I begin to feel my *life* and all of its turning. The *entirety* of my existence, of my consciousness – from before I was born and far beyond the time I die.

I hasten and multiply the eternal rebirth of my Self. In each new moment of this ever-becoming process that I live and make.

Here. Here. Here. Here. Here. Here. Here. This moment is here.

We knew that eventually Percy and the Monster would have to square off. And sure enough, this is exactly what happens in the next song ...

Areas of the MAP are illuminated according to the geographical references.

MONSTER:
Chuska Mountains, I'll never forget youse.
For centuries I lift among your ponderosa pines.
The Defiance Uplift was my, it was my home.
Snow and sunshine at the, at the same time.

All you can eat herbs and berries.
But take only one tenth of what I found there.
I saw the dirt roads – appear
I felt shy about my footprints
Maybe a little ashamed.

Chuska Mountains
Now I look forward to the next rest stop
At the, at the next rest stop we will eat Ponderosa Steakhouse
Chuska Mountains
I'll wait outside in the parking lot
For you, Maery, bring me Styrofoam cartridge.
I send out the call of love to you
Send out the call of love.

Across the Definance Uplift
Full moon eclipsed in front
Comet with 4 tails in the back
Far off, somebody plays a trumpet
Reach in your pocket and find a chocolate
I know someday you will return my calls across the canyon.

MAERY:
The way you move, baby, is so crazy
The way you move, baby, makes everybody crazy – who sees you
You squat all down and move with bent legs
Then you stand up and everybody freaks out

MONSTER:
Clark County, you were formed out of Crawford County
And Dionysus was born out of, born out of Jupiter's legthigh
Ten percent decrease in population in a ten-year span
Wabash River, always the most famous in Indiana

I know you in Illinois, too. Muddy and slow-moving,
I am not deterred. I'll circle fishcampsite til morning.
Squeeze your buttchunk thigh meat, touch you through
the tent.

MAERY:
I heard you were skulking around in the trees by the lake
At the Prairie Band of Potawatomi Nation Reservation
Scooting across the greens, bungling their bison program
Listening in on their community meeting. I hope you went
And did some chores for them in the meantime.

MONSTER:
Chuska Mountains, I'll never forget youse.
For centuries I lift among your ponderosa pines.

Across the Definance Uplift
Full moon eclipsed in front
Comet with 4 tails in the back
Far off, somebody plays a trumpet
Reach in your pocket and find (there) a chocolate
I know someday you will return my calls across the canyon.

Percy re-appears and joins in the song.

PERCY:
Or maybe I'd be ... more like ... a man with a Masters Degree
from Yale AND from Vermont College,
and a teacher at
Vermont College.

For twenty years, hm?
And have published books?
Fiction? And non-fiction?
Having participated in both public and private expeditions and
even organizing expeditions here and there, now and then ....
Hm?
Would I appeal to you more then, Maery?

*Maery groans. The Monster screams and howls but doesn't leave.
Instead, he confronts Percy and things escalate.*

*The Lady Duke enters and is seen surreptitiously examining the
previous scene at the Interstate Rest Stop. She finds and fingers
the broken pieces of the busted Box Desk, examines them, and
begins collecting them.*

LADY DUKE:
For Archival Purposes only. For Marketing Purposes. For
Quality Assurance.
It's safer for everyone this way. Safety first. For safekeeping.
For keeping everything safe. For keeps.

*Underneath the following song, she finds and gathers together the
remains of Maery's makeshift Box Desk and makes a phone call
from the Interstate Rest Area Pay Telephone.*

LADY DUKE:
Halloah? I'd like to register a report. I've had a sighting. Yes,
you might say an encounter. A "Class 'A'."
(*Looking down at the collected pieces of Maery's Box, chuckles*)
Yes, as a matter of fact, I do have some concrete evidence. Some
samples ... that I've collected ...

She checks her watch, and the skies, for the weather pattern, and carries the pieces of the Box Desk elsewhere.

Meanwhile, Maery sings again from the left-hand column, but this time her warbling soprano is supported from underneath by the sonorous, passionate, and paternal bass/countertenor of the Monster in the far right column. He alternates between singing and screaming threateningly and menacing Percy. Percy's pushy tenor maintains his claim on the center-right column, cracking and busting open in effort.

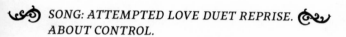 **SONG: ATTEMPTED LOVE DUET REPRISE.** **ABOUT CONTROL.**

MAERY:	PERCY:
Have	possess
Wish	desire, purpose
Caused	derive their origin from
A painting	a representation

MONSTER:
(Singing)
It's hard to think about what you wanted.

(Singing)
the other

MONSTER:
(Speaking)
These guys who bring all the science technology to try and catch and define me. Gimme a break.

safe

Bear to part   be persuaded to part

Eyes were shut to   eyes were insensible to

                                        MONSTER:
                                        (*Singing*)
                        It's hard to think about what you know.

It was a long time   a considerable period elapsed

                                        MONSTER:
                                        (*Speaking*)
            Knock yourself out with your menstrual gorilla urine gauze
            pads on fishhooks, and then you're just going to urinate off the
                porch. Your pheromone and radio chip sandwich. Please.

                                        (*Singing*)
                        This doesn't have to be the big get even.

How my disposition and
habits were altered   the alteration of perceptible in my
                               disposition and habits

                                        MONSTER:
                                        (*Speaking*)
            Biopsy bullets. Three or four planeloads of equipment to the
            remote cabin I keep attacking. Thermal camera traps – primers
                made especially for small fragments of unknown DNA
                                fragments. Heh.

(*Singing*)
This doesn't have to be anything at all.

(*Speaking*)
Six nights have passed, tryin a lot of things boyzzzzzz. Yet
again, morning comes without incident.
You white man think you can prove or disprove my existence
using technology like science or Christianity. And that. Makes
me laugh. HA HA HAHH! But I'm finding my way. From
state to state. On the interstate.

(*Looking at the now dark horizon*)

New Jersey, huhn?

⟨ PART 3 ⟩

THE NKNOTTING

Then, earth began
to bellow, trees
to dance
And howling dogs in glimmering light advance
Ere Hecate came.

- The Aeneid

18. DORIS DUKE RESIDENCY

On the ticker tape video:

So, yes. The Monster has arrived in Somerset County, NJ. It's a heavily populated state, but he finds a suitable habitat, and shelter, at the estate of The Lady Jane Doris Duke ... about the grounds, and also in the unused portion of her home. She senses his presence, as many do before they have a sighting.

WITNESS 1: After we got into the car my cousin, still very petrified, stated that when she was behind the pine trees, something about 5 feet away from her pulled back a branch on one of the trees as if to get a better look at her.

WITNESS 2: I am not the type to believe anything unless i have seen it myself. I know what i seen. Cant explain what it was, but it was alive and real.

WITNESS 1: My uncle stated just as he got to the door something screamed and growled at him. He said the hair on the back of his neck and on his arms stood up, and he ran to his pickup and got the Heck out of there!

WITNESS 2: I heard about an older couple taking a walk in the woods about 3 miles southwest from this area around 3 years ago and they were chased out of the woods by a large hairy man waving a stick and making unusual noises at them.

LADY DUKE:
There were a couple of different ways it happened – was
brought about. This is the first:
(*Songspeak over music*)

THE LADY DUKE FIRST SONGSPEAK OVER MUSIC

I was standing in the ruins of the grand terrarium.
Of course remembering its former splendor,
I could still sweep up a little
let the place know that I still cared.
Distinct feeling of being watched.
Late fall no leaves on the trees.
Dried ivy and dead
still green
still climbed
its columns, leaves languishing
downward.
Outside on the grounds,
blue spruces.

Didn't see anything at first. In fact,
I never saw anything.
Until I saw something.

That's when the smell hit me.
Terrible mildew and filthy animal
New York in August times one thousand.
Hair on the back of my neck.
Almost choked with fear.
How I knew that I was still living.
I still had a body, for oftentimes I am not sure.

The Monster bellows and howls.

Lady Jane Doris Duke runs toward us with her hands over her ears.

LADY DUKE:
That is not a moose or a wolf or a wildcat, or a human!
Something much larger and with a lot more lungpower. My
God! It's echoing through the canyons, the valleys, the gulches,
the gulleys, galleys, the galleries, the hollows, the corridors, the
porticoes, the lobbies!

MONSTER:
That's me. Making choices.
The light coming through was from cracks in the plywood that
board up the windows – not from the stained glass beveled lead
crystal windows of the part where the Duke lived. The Duke?
A lady Duke. Classy lady. Collector. Of the fine, "foreign," and
rare. I think her name was Jane, like Jane, or Doris.

LADY DUKE:
The entire experience is very difficult to put into words. Or
poetry. Or song.

MONSTER:
That's why everybody always says the same words. Almost
always the same words. Your language is limited. Not a lot of
spiritual capacity left in your language.

LADY DUKE:
I knew no one would believe me, so I never talked about it.

WITNESS 2: I am not wanting fame or any TV time.

WITNESS 2: I guess like most people I'm a bit reluctant in
mentioning this but I have to tell someone.

WITNESS 2: She preferred to remain anonymous.

WITNESS 2: I really don't want my name mentioned, we do live in a small community.

WITNESS 2: She was hesitant to tell about her encounter but was talked into reporting this incident by her sister.

WITNESS 2: PLEASE DO NOT POST THIS INFORMATION, THIS IS A SECURE RESIDENCE FOR THE ELDERLY.

WITNESS 2: I was reluctant to make my finding public. Now that I am retired I no longer have such feelings.

MONSTER:
A lot of people don't want to talk about it. There's a weird shame that comes with it. But I appreciate the attempt. And I like your style.

LADY DUKE:
There was ... SOMETHING living in the unused portion of my home. And making its way around the grounds at night. Twisting the limbs off of distant poplars and hurling them at the windowed glass of the conservatory! And whatever it was, we just could not go on this way anymore.

The Lady Duke can hear the Monster heckling a television program about Bigfoot researchers in the unused portion of her home.

LADY DUKE:
This next bit of business alludes to the second way it happened / was brought about. Then we'll return to the first, but this will come back later so don't forget it. Fear not the Primal Layers!

She begins refurbishing the remains of the Box Desk into a large "dresser" and shoves it up against the door to the unused portion of her home.

MONSTER:
(Not having heard the racket because the television set is turned up so loud)
And these guys. You guys are a bunch o' tools. Who do I choose to appear to. THINK ABOUT IT, BRAH: two women. Ojibwe women. A hundred miles to the southeast, picking blueberries and rice.

All of this that the Monster is saying he is now saying in a dark room to the flicker and flash of a television program that shines in his face. We only see it through one of the windows.

MONSTER:
(Cont'd)
Yeah get out your maps, you booger-hunters. Move your base. Snelgrove Lake to Grassy Narrows, eh? Review the whole thing AGAIN before the commercial break – draw it out and keep em watchin. Cause you know what? You got nothin. Yeah, talk to their brother. There's a word for that in Ojibwe – it's called "coming up empty handed." Dopes.

LADY DUKE:
But truly, truly what happened was, that I saw the light from his television in the part of the main house that I wasn't using. And I heard him. Making disparaging remarks to it. What was I to do? I knew I had to confront him now.

MONSTER:
Well, except for this one guy. The guy with the long hair, who knows the woods. He's using his intuition, he's a skeptic, but he's feeling still his way through it. He knows that the feeling of fear points to something bigger than just "stay out of the forest" or "fight back."

LADY DUKE:
And ... and ... also ... I agreed! With what he is saying. It's part
of the reason why my foundation gives so much money to
the arts. Because those ways of knowing get swept under
the carpet.
I ... I don't mean to preach. I don't want this to be about that.

MONSTER:
Mosta you guys at least know not to shoot at me. Oh, wait
hang on. Rewind that part where they talk about how it's kind
of disappointing they didn't see anything. This whole long
weekend and all the money they spent ... the – the BUDGET.
Ah, yeah. I love that.

LADY DUKE:
What I can do, is walk the forest paths. I'll bring my dogs. I'll
explore and be gentle at the same time. I'll help humanity, but
really quietly, as quietly, but stylishly as possible.

MONSTER:
Sounds good. See you on the other side.

LADY DUKE:
What? Hello??

WITNESS 2: The whole time the dogs back hair was raised and
they would not leave our sides.

WITNESS 2: I had taken some friends to our property to do
some coon hunting. These guys had good dogs but when we
tried to turn them loose that would not go out of our sight and
all 3 dogs returned to us within ten minutes and would not
hunt, which was unheard of with these particular dogs.

*The Lady Duke confronts the Monster living in the unused part
of her home, ever so gently, with a post-it note. She addresses the*

dresser which has been pushed in front of the door to the unused house portion. We can no longer see inside the room itself in which the Monster crouches.

LADY DUKE:
I've decided the well-timed post-it note is a nice mode of gentle confrontation. Excuse me ... I beg your pardon. But is someone .... or something .... here?

MONSTER:
(Counter-addressing her from behind the dresser, unseen)
Yes, come in. If you can. If you can move whatever's blocking the door. What is that by the way a chiffarobe?

The Lady Duke glances sidelong at the audience.

MONSTER:
(Cont'd)
I have been living in this unused portion of your home. You have helped me so much.

LADY DUKE:
Those were the words which were spoken to me. It was in a different language, sounding phonetically like Japanese, but it wasn't Japanese. It was like "huuu gob gob muytail grrr ughn."

She screams. Lights out.

LADY DUKE:
(*Songspeak to music*)
Terrified, I ran out and down the staircase.
Pried open the boards
over the side entrance
outside

(*And then again with the songspeak as we arrive at the
Greenhouse of the Formal Gardens*)
to the Japanese garden part
terrarium on the grounds.
All illuminated in moonlight.
I screamed in terror!!!! The scream lifted to glass ceiling
conservatory,
shattering glass raining shards down upon me.

*A well-placed projection shows the illusion of the glass ceiling's
shattering and raining-down.*

LADY DUKE:
(*In songspeak, cont'd*)
It was at this moment that I changed to an immaterial state
– it's completely possible if you can learn to concentrate in the
right way so don't laugh – and was spared the slicing shards.

MONSTER:
Awh – there goes your credibility, Lady Jane Doris Duke!
Ha ha! It's me! Hello! I am a large angry male and I have
followed you! I could be anywhere right now but I'm HERE
– loping across the grounds very quickly on all fours and
crashing through the trees as only I can do. I twist the branch

of a poplar off a tree and hurl it at the building made all of
windows. More shattering. Then I run away back off into the
woods. My residency is over.

LADY DUKE:
No, it isn't.

MONSTER:
Lady Duke. If you come looking for me, your trained attack
dogs will not go with you. If they think they can raise up a
barking search party and step to me I will hurl them through
the air, send them skidding and scampering, whimpering
back to the house, the yard, the truck, the campsite, ears low,
trembling, tails between legs. You will have to come alone.

LADY DUKE:
Hmmm...

She looks at her watch.

MONSTER:
(*Aside*)
So, all this to say, that I wasn't just watching TV in the
abandoned part of the Lady Duke's house.
Watching TV and reading too.
You might already know
– all the classics,
Descartes and Spinoza.
You people are missing two things.
Reverence for the fire
you stole from the gods, and
Justice
the only thing protecting you and all your buddies
from that fire.
I'm no Zeus in telling you this.
I'm not the Prometheus.

Though I'm not Modern, either.

There's more than one way to arrive at a Hillsborough Township "preserved" natural area ...

He roars horribly and seizes a nearby woodpile, shaking it violently. In two easy strides he obtains the Witness Station and destroys it. With a nearly unimaginable, savage fury.

LADY DUKE:
Uhhmm ...

The Lady Duke repairs to one of the greenhouses that has not been destroyed. We then meet a new Witness who we have not yet had the pleasure ...

WITNESS 3: My grandfather worked from the late 1950s to the early '70s as a landscaper on the Duke Estate in Somerset, NJ. When he told this story to my sister and me, he was foggy when giving the exact dates, but he was still very sharp and explained it with incredible detail. My grandfather's job was to manicure and care for the lawns in the north section of the property (whatever that meant) and other various duties. He said that in the summer of 1972, one August afternoon, he was told by the head groundskeeper that he would be working overtime and that he was needed because a shipment was being delivered from Wisconsin. They needed about eight men to unload a crate and to bring it into the garden area.

LADY DUKE:
(In an Exclusive Interview, smoking a cig)
It was in 1964 when I opened "DUKE GARDENS," an extensive and wide-ranging collection of plants from around the world, here at Duke Farms, my home in Hillsborough, New Jersey.

WITNESS 3: When the truck pulled up, my grandfather said that the crate was about 8 feet tall and 5 feet wide.

LADY DUKE:
Duke Gardens included 11 unique gardens which were opened to the public for visitors to enjoy.

WITNESS 3: When he asked what was inside it, the one in charge said they were exotic trees.

LADY DUKE:
While tours are by appointment, anyone can apply to see the gardens. Anyone!

WITNESS 3: What happened next was enough to make half of the team get up and walk off the job, and not care about the consequences.

LADY DUKE:
In the 1970s, also at Duke Farms, I exhibited a complete temple building, that I collected in the 1950s and 1960.

WITNESS 3: When the men started pushing the crate off of the flatbed truck, a blood-curdling scream was unleashed from within the box.

LADY DUKE:
I have always been an avid collector of art, flora, and fauna.

WITNESS 3: While the men were regaining their composure, most of the help walked off the job.

LADY DUKE:
Like my father, I cultivated, hybridized, and propagated orchids, as an example that should show you.

WITNESS 3: They said they didn't want to get hurt or mauled dealing with a wild animal without the proper safety equipment.

LADY DUKE:
The Phalaenopsis Doris, registered by Duke Farms in 1940, is a milestone in white Phalaenopsis breeding.

WITNESS 3: So off they went, including my grandfather.

LADY DUKE:
I have two Bactrian camels, Baby and Princess, who reside at both the Rough Point and Duke Farms estates.

WITNESS 3: What the two remaining men witnessed that night was enough to make them seek employment elsewhere.

LADY DUKE:
Baby and Princess were part of a purchase of a Boeing 737-300 from a Middle Eastern businessman.

WITNESS 3: The tale of what they witnessed was relayed to my grandfather by the two men, and he relayed it to us as children.

LADY DUKE:
(*Sidenote*)
(I bought the aerocraft to accommodate my continuing love of travel and my desire for privacy.)

WITNESS 3: My grandfather stuck by his story until the very end.

LADY DUKE:
And when we had a hurricane at Rough Point, I had straw spread out on the ballroom floor and Baby and Princess came inside.

WITNESS 3: About two weeks before he passed away, my sister reminded me to bring it up again and confront him, which I did.

LADY DUKE:
I want these things to be near me, these unusual and singular creatures and creations that would seem strange and exotic to others –

WITNESS 3: Grandpa, remember the crate you had to move in New Jersey? Did you embellish at all? Because now would be the time to tell me.

LADY DUKE:
I *must* have them near me, I must *have* them, and I must *keep* and *feeeed* and *protect* them.

WITNESS 3: He looked at me and said, "You want to know if I embellished the story. The truth is that I am guilty of the opposite."

LADY DUKE:
The exploration of collecting them is what defines my universe and gives my life meaning. And protects me from *unpleasantness.*

WITNESS 3: He said, "There was so much that I left out ...the story was just the beginning.

LADY DUKE:
And it's the same with art, the creations – the crea-tures! – of the artists! Creations! Crea-tures!

WITNESS 3: "Remember something," he said to me, looking me straight in the eye, "I worked there for two more years after that," he said, "There are things that a young mind should not hear."

LADY DUKE:
Of the great *geniuses* who work in and among our very souls as

the forces of nature work in and among all that lives and grows!

WITNESS 3: I said, "But I am not a child anymore. I am sure I can handle what it is that you have to say."

LADY DUKE:
It is up to me to *collect* and *keep* these *rare* and *precious* creations – ! To shelter them from the cruelty of the world!

WITNESS 3: Grandfather said, "Tomorrow I will finish the story. Come back tomorrow."

LADY DUKE:
For the world.

WITNESS 3: But there was no tomorrow.

LADY DUKE:
For the future.

WITNESS 3: Grandfather passed away at 2 a.m. that morning in a New York hospital.

LADY DUKE:
And for the sake of the future!

19. INTERVIEW with a FINALIST

On the Ticker Tape:

Lights up on a more civilized section of the Formal Gardens, where Maery learns from The Lady Duke that she is a finalist for a major award. This award would put an end her financial woes for good. But it comes at a high cost, for she also learns that The Lady Duke has collected her Box of Keepsakes. And with it ... her most important creation ...

Maery and The Lady Duke sit at a desk.

LADY DUKE:
Maery, I've reviewed your application for The Lady Jane Duke Artist Award and I must say that you make a very strong case. Normally I have the selection committee review the applications, but in this case I wanted to have a look myself. And I'm ever so glad I did. I'm especially interested in your Afro Gothic Manifesto. And I quote: "Gothic narratives were

MAERY:
"(and still are) a means of working through the discomfort of a changing world through the safety of fiction: fears of industrialization, the speed of scientific discovery, the uncertainty of secularism, epidemics and disease, immigrants, and cultural others, nuclear annihilation, climate change ...

every real social fear has its metaphorical monster.... Blackness in America has not only never been comfortable, but is a constant source of discomfort ... To be the fear, to be the thing that goes bump in the night hiding under the bed. It is one thing to use literature and film to process social anxieties, but what do you do when you are the social anxiety? What do you do when the villagers with torches and pitchforks are coming after you?"[27]

LADY DUKE:
My, my. I'd never thought of it that way!

MAERY:
No, you wouldn't have.

LADY DUKE:
And your perspective is so vital for the credibility of our prestigious cultural institutions at the moment. And I'm a great admirer of your work! It means a great deal to me, alone here at the heady, lonesome peaks of civilized culture ...

MAERY:
Hmph. You know, and I just also want to say that we need more funding for women artists and writers. I don't know a single woman artist that can even live and work successfully under the yoke of male domestic presence which he always forces her into servitude or at least hogs up the intellectual space.

LADY DUKE:
I'm trying to think of an example. I mean, I never felt suppressed.

27. Please note: Mary Shelley did not, in fact, write an Afro Goth Manifesto. And neither did Sibyl Kempson. Leila Taylor is the author quoted here, from her excellent memoir and stirring cultural critique *Darkly: Black History and America's Gothic Soul*, London: Repeater Books, 2019.

MAERY:
But you were always plentiful of funds and vast fortunes of
your own! You're not the one working in the freezing cold
Berlin attic wrapping the clay and the wet rags around the
rusty iron frame. You're not spending your life's blood making
thousands of tiny paintings in black and white paint that
never sell.

LADY DUKE:
I do certainly see your point.

MAERY:
If somebody tells you that a woman is living a fulfilled life as
an artist and also is living with a man, then that somebody is
either lying or being lied to.
And I do love you, Lady Jane Williams Doris Duke. We all do.
So highly appreciative and spiritual, your natural grace and
beauty, always learning the higher learning. The Shangri-La is
ever in our hearts.
Deep down we are just two women looking out to sea after the
storm, searching the horizon for some sign of a boat. We are
looking for the same boat.

*The Lady Duke becomes Jane Williams for a moment. They stare
out at the relentless and reticent sea for some moments.*

MAERY:
Any news?

JANE:
... No. No news.

*They manage to retain the tranquilizing spell of mutual
unbeknownst widowhood for a few moments, and the atmosphere
grows heavy and misty with sorrow.*

Then it dissipates, and we are back to the previous discussion.

MAERY:
But.

LADY DUKE:
But what about Mrs. Wills for you.

MAERY:
She's a help but mostly we can only afford to ask her to work for us from beyond the grave. I tell you I would have been better off alone. You'll notice that "domestic" and "dominate" have the same Latin root. I go to lengths to point that out in my artist statement.

LADY DUKE:
I did read that, yes. An excellent, valid point. Except slightly that it isn't quite true. They're two different words from two different roots.

MAERY:
Humph. And how does that actually matter?

LADY DUKE:
Touché.

Maery lights up a cigarette in a finger-ring holder.

LADY DUKE:
That'll be 50 cents, Maery S.

MAERY:
Oh, right.

Hands it over from her coinpurse.

LADY DUKE:
Thank you very much. I'm just going to keep it here for you,
for safekeeping. I should say you've got a very good chance at
an award this year, and so I'm hoping this'll all go back into
your own coinpurse and then some.

MAERY:
Nice of you to say, Lady Duke.

LADY DUKE:
Maery, what about the tribes? The Germanic tribes. Didn't you
have a great success there at one time?

MAERY:
Nearly.

LADY DUKE:
Ceramic arts, wasn't it?

MAERY:
Well, yes. More like smashing ceramics. Glueing googly eyes
on them and then smashing. More like performance art. I still
think about it and it makes me feel ravenous, like I could eat
anything and it would just burn up in my belly. Scrap metal,
a shit-ton of cheeseburgers, the anger and judgments of others
– injustice even. Sometimes it feels like I'm devouring and
incinerating the interstate in the same way. (O, but I've GOT to
find that Box of mine – those Keepsakes!)

LADY DUKE:
Hmm?

She places the original Box Desk of Keepsakes on the table.

MAERY:
Why – YOU! How do YOU have it!?

LADY DUKE:
I've collected it.

MAERY:
My identity! My credibility! My belonging!

LADY DUKE:
It's been part of my collection since 1948. It's safe here with
me. It's so, so safe here. What would you do with it anyway,
if you had it? Maery, I've followed you // through the bleakest
reaches of German Romanticism, Dark Romanticism, through
the unforgiving cliffs /// and bluffs above the Rhine, into the
annals of pulsating Goth and Afro Goth subcultures, picked up
the pieces of this degraded Box of yours –

MAERY:
// You've been following me!

MAERY:
/// The cliffs! The bluffs! The twisty foot-routes!

MAERY:
(*Darkly*)
Broken on the beach,
smashed on the shoals, on the – on the rocky shores,
along the blind alleys, the backwoods misty thickets,
the rest stop dumpsters along the Interstate,
from among the discarded art school refuse,
the jumbled typefaces from rusty, abandoned printing
presses, the arching ruins of Gothic architectures –
ogival and revival alike,
scattered among the diagonal groins and ribs of the vaults ... !

LADY DUKE:
That's right. I merely gathered up what you'd been forced
to leave behind and lost, all the things you didn't have the

resources or the wherewithal to carry with you or care for properly – for you were always so busy working and making, consorting with your creation, your crea-ture.

Which is how it should be, Maery! The artist must be free to continue to create!

MAERY:
But I'll never be able to buy that back from you! I don't have that kind of money – and anyway my checquebook's in there! It's almost everything I have!

LADY DUKE:
Well. Almost.

Pause. Maery suddenly understands. The corners of The Lady Duke's smile tremble greedily, victoriously, perniciously. Maery's eyes grow wide in disbelief and panic.

LADY DUKE:
For Archival Purposes. For Marketing Purposes.
For Quality Assurance.
(*Aside*)
This is the second way it happened.

(*To Maery*)
It's your identity, your heritage, your ancestry that is most valuable to me and the endowment. There's a veritable gold rush going on for narratives such as yours, and I'm a prospector. Your branding is the crown jewel for my branding. I must have it for my foundation. And for safety's sake. For safekeeping. For keeps.

The Lady Duke holds up some scraps of testimony from Witness 2:

WITNESS 2: I dont know that I am able to do justice to be able to tell you the way I felt at that moment.

WITNESS 2: I was so scared that it instantly made me cry.

WITNESS 2: Never have I been so scared by something in the woods that I have cried. I have come face to face with bear and elk and mountain lion. I was scared in those situations too, but not like this. When it let out that yell/scream was what really touched a fear in me.

LADY DUKE:
(*Looking at her watch, standing, pushing the Box Desk closer to the center of the little table that sits between them*)
If you'll excuse me a moment. I'm expecting a shipment. From Wisconsin. Some exotic trees for the garden. Arriving in a large crate, on the rear of a large transport vehicle which is very late in arriving. There must be traffic out on the Parkway, unless they're coming through Flemington which these days there could be plenty of traffic certainly there as well ... Some of the groundskeepers and landscape workers have been asked to stay late and work overtime. I want to stay and oversee, from a safe distance ...

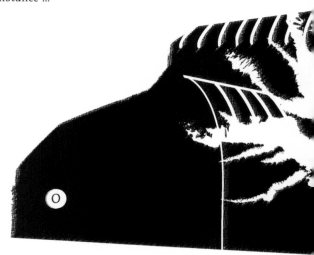

Maery places a single hand on the top of the Box Desk. She turns to see the arrival of the Truck, which carries an identical, but larger-scale (much larger-scale) version of the Box Desk carried atop a trailer on the back of the Truck.

LADY DUKE:
And anyway, Maery, just look. Your identity, in my care, has become so much larger now than you can ever carry in your own life or self. That is what the achievement of a masterpiece can do, you see, to a person. To a woman.
You are beyond identity now, beyond persona. You're an icon, an image, an idol! You've entered the realm of myth, my dear. You are an archetype in the Mythic Order.

MAERY:
(*Slamming her fist onto her Box, startling The Lady Duke*)
I always WAS!!!!!

The restored and refurbished Box is cracked once again.

Based on a real internet story, the Monster is brought to the Duke estate – drugged, shackled to a rocking chair, and pent up in a crate. He has been collected.

During the following song, the Witnesses return to their Witness Station to find it destroyed. They sadly gather up the Box and remaining keepsakes as best they can.

 SONG: 'EXOTIC TREE' DELIVERY,
OF THOSE WHO BEAR WITNESS

That night
The truck
Getting late
Eight men eager, to get the job overwith
Be on their way, be on their way
What happened next?

What happened next
Walk off the job
Not care the consequences
Be on their way, be on their way
What happened next?

Two men remain
Get the load
Drag it toward the garden

Be on their way, be on their way
What happened next?

What the two remaining
I am telling you now
Seek employment elsewhere
How it told me

Be on their way, be on their way. What happened next? (x3)
How it told me.

During the singing of the Song of Those Who Bear Witness, The Lady Jane Doris Duke has kept watch out of an upper story window, smoking a cig.

LADY DUKE:
Needless to say, I was played by Lauren Bacall in my very own miniseries about me. It was aired on NBC. The National Broadcast Coalition.

The Crate, which is the larger replica of the Box Desk and the Dresser, is wheeled along the gravel pathway of the Formal Gardens, on a dolly guided by two Groundskeeper/Witnesses. The same crack that has appeared on Maery's Box appears on the Crate. It topples and falls to its side, revealing the Monster. Witness 3 continues, taking over the Testimonies.

WITNESS 3: While guiding the crate down the main path, balance was lost and the crate came off the wheels. The crate hit hard enough to crack the side of the crate and loosen the side panel, which fell off and exposed the contents.

Shackles on its arms and legs and feet. Lying on its side, but tied
to a rocking chair. A water bottle is nailed to the side of the 'Crate'
which is the back of the Dresser, near the creature's head.
An IV stand connected to the wall of the dresser/crate and
stuck to its arm.

WITNESS 3: Inside the crate sat a creature that had the shape of
a man, but was anything but a man. The face didn't look like a
man, but had some human features.

The inside of the crate is plastered with Collected Witness
Testimonies, and the empty husks of Ghosted Children.

The creature tries to speak or communicate with words, but all it
does is keep on drooling.

The Groundskeeper/Witnesses back away quickly.

WITNESS 3: One of the oddest parts to this story was that
my grandfather was told that this creature was sitting on a
rocking chair! I could never understand this. After thinking
about it, though, I think it was maybe to prevent this "thing"
from getting cramps during the move.

The phone rings in the ruins of the Witness Station.
It rings and rings.

The Lady Duke approaches with an embroidered towel and
crouches before the creature, gently wiping away some of the drool.

LADY DUKE:
You are home. Welcome home. Welcome home, my dear friend
and darling. Welcome home.

He is trying to speak. He is trying to say, "DON'T YOU KNOW
THE LAND IS WATCHING YOU?"
"SHIZEN WA GENGODESU, ANATA WA YOMU KOTO GA

DEKIMASEN KA?"
"MAE NATUR YN IAITH, ONI ALLWCH CHI DDARLLEN?"
"NATUR IST EINE SPRACHE, KANNST DU NICHT LESEN?"
But he is too heavily drugged.

MONSTER:
Gob gob muytail grr grr, gob gob,
gob gob muytail ughn ughn.
Gob gob. Gob gob.

The lights fade on the pair.

OVER-THE-PHONE WITNESS 2: These sounds I heard had a
structure and I felt like it was a language of some kind.

The telephone rings and it's The Lady Jane Doris Duke calling
for Maery.

LADY DUKE:
Hello, Maery, I've finally got some news! I'm so pleased
to be able to tell you that you've been selected. You have
been selected.

MAERY:
"The Veil is torn now."

Maery tells her before hanging up.

21. EPILOGUE, PATERSON, NJ.

Enter Maery S. and Company gradually into the yard of a hillside. The Monster sings from an airport in Newark, NJ, hoping to travel far, far away. During his song – or, really Emmylou Harris's song, Maery repairs and polishes her Box of Keepsakes.

 SONG: BOULDER TO BIRMINGHAM, REMIX

MONSTER:
I don't wanna hear a lovesong
I got on this airplane just to fly //
I know there's life below me
But all that you can show me
Is the prairie and the sky

I don't want to hear a sad story
full of heartbreak and desire.
The last time I felt like this
I was in the wilderness and the canyon was on fire
And I stood on a mountain in the night
And I watched it burn. I watched it burn. I watched it burn.

MAERY:
// I keep catching myself looking for you – everywhere now,
and you don't appear to me any longer. Crossing the hills above

the highway – 68 or 64 – behind the tractor dealer? Just along the tree line? But you are nowhere.

On the Ticker Tape, describing the action: Clarie and Fanny, both turned to Peasant (mer)Maids in death, build a fire in a short barrel behind the house. The ghost of Percy Shelley brings out some potatoes, dragging their bag behind him through the fallen leaves, and they bake them on the flames, sitting on boxes, in the wind from the other hill. Squishy squid tentacles and tendrils spill out slightly from the tails of his frockcoat, and as he sits at the fire a black liquid oozes down the crate on which he sits. He must needs keep his face turned slightly from the flames lest they dry his facial tentacles out. No great or famous river is any longer visible, unless you count the meandering Passaic, which is the only body of water within sight in this particular view of Paterson, NJ.

LB IN GHOSTLY FORM:
You can stay inside your RV
watch the episodes of Nova or the History Channel
that will do an attempt at a dramatised re-enactment for you.
But that isn't going to tell you who they were.
(*He looks down at the meandering Passaic*)
Ahh, the meandering Passaic. It ain't the Rhine, that's for sure.

He shakes everyone's hand, and lifts a tentacle of Percy's and shakes that (they are weak and useless out of water). LB paints, in bright temperas, a banner that says "200th Year Reunion – Class of 1819."

LB IN GHOSTLY FORM:
Paterson, NJ. The meandering Passaic. From Somerset County, NJ it's a journey of 44 miles up the Garden State Parkway. 59 minutes in current traffic. Or 47 minutes if you take Route 80 and 287.

THE VOICE OF THE MONSTER:
Ugh. I hate 287.

Everyone turns, except for Maery, to look behind them, but no one is there.

In the corner of the bottom of the ruined Box of Keepsakes, is one lonesome, quivering Witness Testimony, stuck in the corner by a sticky old dried wad of chewing gum speckled with flecks of pipe tobacco.

WITNESS 2: When I asked her how she felt about the experience she told me it was hard to describe. The awe that came over her was different than what they felt when seeing local wildlife, describing it as disbelief and excitement at the same time.

And so they adjust to their new era, nearly all of which remains yet unclear.

MONSTER:
(*Singing*)
I would rock my soul in the bosom of Abraham
I would hold my life his saving grace
I would walk all the way from Boulder to Birmingham
If I thought I could see, I could see your face.

Well, you really got me this time
And the hardest part is knowing
I'll survive ...

The Very End